Starfire: Memory's Blade

ALSO BY SPENCER ELLSWORTH

Starfire: A Red Peace
Starfire: Shadow Sun Seven

STARFIRE
MEMORY'S BLADE
SPENCER ELLSWORTH

A TOM DOHERTY ASSOCIATES BOOK
NEW YORK

STARFIRE: MEMORY'S BLADE

Cover illustration by Sparth
Cover design by Christine Foltzer

Edited by Beth Meacham

A Tor.com Book
Published by Tom Doherty Associates
175 Fifth Avenue
New York, NY 10010

www.tor.com

Tor® is a registered trademark of
Macmillan Publishing Group, LLC.

ISBN 978-0-7653-9576-4 (ebook)
ISBN 978-0-7653-9577-1 (trade paperback)

First Edition: February 2018

To my children. A small stroke in the fight
to make the future worthy of you.

The Empire would have you believe that the war against the Shir is, by definition, endless. The Shir are evil and insentient, so the solution is to have them fight soldiers who are good, and insentient. War is a thing done by the Great Other. Principles of Empire fall apart if you assume not one, but two basic facts:

1. That "crosses," meaning constructed soldiers, are inherently sentient.

2. That the Shir are also inherently sentient, if alien.

The average citizen, colonized by Jorian legends and half-truths embodied in scripture, cannot accept either. It would mean that every vegetable on their plate, every bolt of cloth, every breath of sweet terraformed air, is paid for over and over again in the blood of a sentient being meant for disposal.

—**John Starfire,** *Toward a New Sentience*

God's hand stretches over the galaxy, and the stars shift, the planets align. The son of stars and the children of giants battle on the paths through the dark. The children shall be the change, and the change shall be the children.

—**First Book of Joria**

Starfire: Memory's Blade

Entr'acte

A BLACK THREAD CAME out of space and touched the sun in the Aria system.

Aria was a wild world, far from Imperial control. Populated by miners on its moon and asteroids, obscure religionists in its one vast desert, and coastal homes for those rich enough to hire private security, it had never been a pleasant place. The single huge continent made for terrible weather. The rocky moons had poor magnetic fields and wouldn't take to terraforming, and the ocean, no matter how often new processing spores were introduced, was too acidic to support water-going sentients. Many wondered why the Jorians, eight thousand years ago, had bothered to terraform Aria in the first place.

But for three billion sentients, Aria's one desert continent, acidic seas, and mining operations were home.

As is so common with home, few noticed that something was different when a dark spot grew on the sun.

Two days before the end, one of the cultists looked up and thought he saw a black spot on the sun. This believer had pushed himself to sojourn in the desert, despite the fact that his people were native water-dwellers, and only by crossing their genes with humans had they been able to make themselves durable enough to live at least part of their lives on land. He was sick, skin cracking, pores bleeding, his tentacles shriveled, but he continued through the desert to test his flagging faith.

Looking up, he saw the black spot on the sun. At first he attributed it to the lack of water, and begged his gods for strength. But after drinking from a spring and eating a few morsels of his meager food, he still saw it.

He returned to his people to tell them that the end was coming—the stars were going out. And they studied their books and referenced their prophecies and decided it was true. They fasted. They prayed. They commended him on his faith, to see what they had been too busy to notice.

They did not inform the territorial authority, who considered them a nuisance.

Had they informed the territorial authority, that minor official would have likely done nothing, filed no report. On the off chance a report was filed, had the report been read by anyone in power, most likely the phenomena would not have been recognized as what it was. By some miracle, had it been recognized for what it was, someone in the territorial authority might have petitioned the Imperial Navy.

But there was no more Imperial Navy. Irithessa was in flames, the Emperor was dead, and John Starfire and the Resistance were hunting out every human they could find. They called it the Red Peace, for the blood spilled. That sort of trouble was what sent people to places like Aria.

The asteroid miners noticed, on the third day by Imperial reckoning. Their manager assumed it was some kind of flare-up, and called the parent company to send a team of solar monitors. This was a stable sun, and there should have been no risk of severe flares or solar destabilization.

One of the asteroid miners shook and muttered prayers and swore they had to leave. She was a grizzled miner from a long-lived species, distrusted by the others for her strange gods and her strange ways. They didn't listen to her—at first. When she refused to work, they locked her in the brig.

On the morning of the fourth day, another black thread crossed the space between the sun and Aria.

The black thread touched down in an algae-thick ocean. It sent ripples of yellow lightning through the sky and black veins through the water.

The storms and subsequent waves destroyed the coasts of the continent. An earthquake swallowed the religious colony, and he who had seen the dark spot on the sun had only a few seconds to ponder this fulfillment of faith before he fell into an abyss.

The center of Aria's one continent bubbled open and vomited darkness and slag. The atmosphere roiled with toxic fumes. No sentient could live on Aria now.

The miners on the asteroid piled into their one node-worthy ship. She who had seen this coming shook and prayed to her forgotten gods, and the others with her did the same.

The only way out was through the system's single faster-than-light node, and that node hung in space just outside Aria's orbit.

With no other choice, the miners flew from the asteroids toward the dead world and the black thread that had come from the sun, praying the devils wouldn't notice one small ship entering the node.

There were only a few hundred of them, thinking of the lives they had back at the company's headquarters, or their home worlds, thinking of mates and children and life.

They reached the node. They punched in their codes, and waited for their node-engines to hum in harmony with the wormhole and waited for the darkness of space to twist and roil and suck them in, and spit them out at the company headquarters in a safe place.

Below them Aria turned red and molten, its clouds superheating and boiling the one massive ocean.

Their ship hummed and the node began to open, slowly, interminably—

And a black thread rose from the planet below and touched their ship.

For just a few moments, they knew.

They heard the gurgle of the ten million eggs that Aria now hosted, the web now spun through what had been a healthy sun, and they felt the hunger, the hunger of the Shir to consume every star, every sentient, every song, and all they could see, looking into that future, was the fierce, consuming hunger, a hunger darker and colder than the emptiest corner of space—

The node caught them, but the black thread held.

Metal screamed, and the atmosphere rushed out, as the opposing forces of pure space and darkness tore the ship apart, and the miners went flying into vacuum, the last sentients in the Aria system to die.

Another black thread spread from the planet.

And another.

1

Jaqi

IT'S HIM.

Standing right in front of me. The ruler of the galaxy. The tyrant and the deliverer. The fella I aim to kill.

I know because I seen the fella on the screens. Seen that sword, right down to the flame symbol of the Resistance carved into the pommel stone, and I have to say, even with the gray in his hair and the wild eyes, and the way he clenches and unclenches his hand on his sword, he's still as handsome as they made him look. A real slab.

John Starfire.

The Usurper, to say what folk been calling him around me.

Here, in front of me, is the man who overthrew the Empire, brought peace and justice to the galaxy.

Unless you're a human, and then he threw you in a death camp.

And here we are, two of us, with swords, standing on a bridge, in an ancient abandoned temple, above an abyss, like a scene from some holo.

He doesn't say anything. Just stares at me. For all he's a cross, his face is unique, most likely fixed up surgical. His hand holds tight to the hilt of his sword, like it's been glued there.

If I can run, and get through the field, my pal Scurv Silvershot will make short work of this fellow pretty quick. Swords en't no use against a couple of shard-blasters that always hit their targets.

But no, the controls for the protective field are in this building somewhere. Scurv is locked out till I figure that.

He finally speaks. "You're just some space scab. Why you?"

"Say what?"

"Why does it talk to you?"

"Why does what talk to me?"

He doesn't answer, just clutches his sword hilt.

Must be talking about that thing. The thing what just seemed to touch me and move away. I don't know how to describe it but to say it was all made up of music. And seemed to have my parents' faces. And then had the face of a devil.

Sounds like nonsense, once I think on it. But it's real—it just wasn't a thing you see with eyes. It's gone now, into the depths of this temple, which stretch away far below this bridge I stand on.

"You still don't get it." He shakes his head. "I went through twenty thousand memory crypts on Irithessa looking for this information. I spent whole weeks just trying to find what you fell into."

I don't know what he's speaking about. I know I can't beat him in a fair fight, so I'd better get him outside. Better find the controls for the field keeping Scurv out.

"Why does it talk to you?"

So I run.

He runs after me. He's fast. Soldier fast, kind of runner that trains for this. All I have is desperation, as I round the end of the bridge, run along another walkway that hugs the wall above this big abyss. I just need to split through one of them hallways that runs off to the side, just need to get outside—

You cannot run! You must face him.

The voice throws me off and I nearly go right over the edge. It's my mother's voice.

"Not you again!" I leap over a piece of metal blocking a dusty hallway, run down the hallway. That *thing* is going and talking to me again, with the voices of my folks!

I bolt down the dusty hallway—and reach a shut steel door with no working pad. It doesn't open when I run right into it. I did get the outside gate to open just with my hand. I try my hand on the scan plate next to the door—but there is none. This door is going to stay closed.

I spin around and face John Starfire. Like an idiot, I grab the sword at my waist, the huge Thuzerian black-bladed sword, and draw it.

I can't think of anything else to do, even though it's a pain just to hold out the heavy thing, and en't no way I'll fight with it.

He stops. "Don't try to fight. Just tell me why it talks to you."

"Why does what talk to—" I break off, because my parents stand behind him.

I know it's fake, but my breath catches in my chest all the same, and the same tears start up from behind my eyes.

There's still a little girl inside me, sure they'll get back from way out in space any day now.

<u>You have to beat him,</u> my parents say.

Well, they don't quite say. It en't quite speech. I can make words out of the impressions, but it feels like music. That crazing music, what Araskar goes on about, the same thing swept through me when I did them "miracles" before. It sounds mad, but there it is—music making meaning out of itself.

The music is what folk call the Starfire, the power that moves through pure space.

And somehow my brain makes it into words, words

coming out of my long-dead folks.

<u>You must stop him,</u> the music says. My parents change, blur together. They become that thing, the thing I saw when I got in, what looked like the devil but was also made of music. <u>You must stop him or else he will bond with us, take us for his own.</u>

"Are you . . ." This can't be true, not a burning thing about it. "Are you the Starfire its own self? You got a voice and you're talking to me? The song of stars, just talking to me?"

The music rushes into my mind with a forceful <u>Yes.</u>

John Starfire stops, hesitates, though he's still holding that sword out like he knows how to use it. "You're speaking to it. How?"

I ignore him and keep speaking to the Starfire itself, which still looks like my parents, but bigger, changing, shifting a thousand colors and sounds, filling me up. "You saying I'm it. I really am this special oogie deliverer of space." Is this it, then? This is all that talk writ down in the Bible, what I can't read, and here I am and despite all my skeptical words, it's coming true? Despite my shaky track record with miracles, it's all true?

John Starfire doesn't respond to that. But *the* Starfire, the stuff of space itself, does. <u>You are the one I have waited for.</u>

Well, shit.

I was well sure I wasn't no Chosen One. The truth was that everything I've done was just trickery with a node. That en't Chosen business.

Except the Starfire itself just told me I am.

It don't get much more Son of Stars than that.

"You don't want to fight me," John Starfire says.

<u>You must stop him,</u> the music counters.

I set my teeth and try spreading my legs. I'm the Son of Stars, and he en't, then mayhap it don't matter that he's the better swordsman. Mayhap it don't matter that Taltus's sword, this heavy Thuzerian thing made of black metal, is already hurting my arm. Mayhap it don't matter, because if fate chose me, then I can beat him.

And when I think that, my sword breaks into blue flame. I remember what Scurv said—*them swords work off faith.*

"I can already tell you have no training." He gives me a real charming smile. "We're both crosses. You have to understand that the humans want us to fight. They've manipulated you. Just tell me why it talks to you, and what I need to do to make it talk to me."

Just need to rush him and stick this big old sword through his vitals, and—and this'll be done. Bill, and Quinn, Taltus and all the other dead will be avenged.

"Don't be their puppet. Don't be stupid."

"Not stupid," I say. "I got destiny on my side."

I rush him.

One second he's in front of me; next he's aside, and strikes my sword with such a blow I near drop it, go stumbling, and then I *do* drop it—I back up against the door and grab it, turn around.

Burning hell, he's quick.

He slashes his hand and the familiar white fire of a cross's soulsword leaps up his blade. He shakes his head. "To think, even I hoped you were more than propaganda."

I pick up my sword and rush him again. Come on, destiny—

This time he just stops me. Doesn't move an inch, knocks me back with the force of his counter-blow. I stumble backward, and my stupid heavy sword drops again, my point screeching on the metal of the floor.

Hell! "Come on, fate!" I say, to whatever's out there. "You even listening?"

He comes toward me now. "I see I have to make you bleed to make you understand," he says. "That's fine. Good, even."

And now he really fights me. And I'm scrambling backward, trying to stay away, because that sword is like a snake about to strike, and I been in some scraps but no one, not even Araskar, moves this quick, this liquid-fast, and suddenly I'm backed up against this closed door and his soulsword knocks mine aside—

He slashes my arm.

Fire shoots through my veins. My sight goes red. I sink to my knees.

Feels like he's ripping tendons out from the inside. But the tendons are my memories, and he *yanks* on my image of my mater and pater, and suddenly it's like the memory is tumbling away from me—I can't recall their faces, and I grab for their faces, and—

"Like I thought, just some scab." He kicks me, and I slam back into the closed door, and my wounded arm won't clutch the soulsword right anymore, so it falls. The blue flame vanishes. "And one who believes every word the humans say."

The music cries and screeches off in the distance.

He knocks me down again, too fast. His soulsword goes right through my leg, pins me to the floor.

He rips those memories apart.

My mater and pater, and Bill's, and waiting there in the darkness for my parents to come back, and then taking odd jobs until I done found the kids—and that gray girl and Bill dies and the kids talking about their memory crypt, Araskar and Trace and the Engineer and Shadow Sun Seven and Scurv—soon as I think these memories, they tear away from me, go spinning like flotsam. They've all come unmoored.

I think I hear my mother singing, but I can't make out the words. It's all white noise.

The Usurper won.

2

Araskar

I STAND WITH A venerable old council of madmen, in a galaxy of madmen.

On the holo-viewer, the Resistance ships get closer.

"They are just beyond Frodigand," says Father Rixinius, the oldest of the Thuzerian Ruling Council. His voice echoes around the ancient stone chamber. Solid rock, this. A nice, solid meeting chamber older than the Second Empire itself.

"What's Frodigand?" I ask.

"The seventh Saint, but for our purposes, the seventh planet in our solar system." He raises a finger at the blinking lights in the holo. The representation of the solar system hangs, in swirling shades of light, above their war table. "There is another node out there. Ruins of a First Empire settlement, but no terraforming. They are giving us time."

"Wow," I say. "A two-node system. Living in luxury."

It's a stupid thing to say, and it gets me more glares

from around the room. But if these folk don't glare at you, you must not be screwing up enough. Everyone in the Thuzerian Ruling Council has been a monk, abstaining from all fun for at least fifty years by Imperial reckoning, sometimes seventy, one hundred—in the case of a few long-lived sentients, one hundred fifty. Everyone in this smelly, old, cold rock chamber that predates the Second Empire.

Military monks, I should clarify. A handful of them even fought in the Dark Zone, and many of them fought against the Empire at some point. Abstaining from everything except violence.

And while I don't know much about religion, I know veterans. Once you've been in battle, you get terribly pragmatic.

They're adding up all the lives they have on the ground, the lives on their ships, versus one life.

Mine.

I look at the readings. "That's five Imperial dreadnoughts. Or Resistance dreadnoughts, maybe we should call them. Slightly smaller than what you have. They'll carry thirty gunships and three hundred Moths each, if it comes down to that."

"So they are keeping the Imperial munitions works running," says another of the Thuzerian council, a woman who sounds almost human, though you can't tell through those masks. "They must be, to mount this attack."

"They've got it all running," I say, from my position on the floor, next to their table. "Full complement. There's no way to crew five whole dreadnoughts without bringing the vats online."

I hear several sharp intakes of breath, from those monks who breathe through a mouth. John Starfire pledged to shut down the vats. If he hasn't, he has an infinite number of new soldiers.

"We must sue for some kind of parley," says Father Rixinius. He's an elderly Grevan, tall and too thin, and to most sentients he looks like a thing out of a nightmare, with those deep-set red-framed eyes, and those incisors that hang over his bottom lip, sticking out from underneath his ceremonial bone mask, carved deep with various curling designs.

"You knew you would have to pick a side."

I turn around to tell Paxin to be quiet, but she's on the other side of the table, somehow managing to look more commanding than me despite her condition.

Paxin is the default leader of the refugees we picked up on our mission to Shadow Sun Seven, a writer whose work helped inspire the Resistance, but had the unfortunate DNA of pure Earth stock, and fell in line with John Starfire's purge of the blueblood humans. Right now she's looking a little better than she was in the mines, but she's still hollow-cheeked and sickly. She coughs into the stump of her right hand, still tries to cover her mouth with fingers the Resistance cut off.

Father Rixinius waits until Paxin's coughing subsides, then says, slowly, "The Masked Faith cannot begin a war with the Resistance, for the same reasons we could not ever truly declare war against the Empire."

"Which reasons are—" Paxin breaks into more coughing.

"Our dreadnoughts are spread out, doing the work of God throughout the galaxy," says Rixinius. "We have called muster, but it will take time for them to return, to gather. It will take time to arm them fully. None of our ships have a full complement of shards, or short-range fighters. The Resistance knows this."

"You have a moral duty. You never took a stand when it mattered," Paxin says. "You never sided with the Empire or the Resistance."

"We also don't own a thousand factory moons!" he growls through that mask.

I wish Jaqi were here. She's good at talking people into crazing things. "It's all right," I say. "There will be no grand military stand. Let me speak."

"I won't let you offer yourself as some sacrifice, Araskar," Paxin says.

"That's nice of you," I say. "Didn't know you know my name."

"Of course I know who you are," Paxin says. "We know all of you who set us free. The seven: you, the Zarra Z and the fallen X, and Kalia and Toq of Formoz, and Jaqi, and—"

"Ai, enough," I say. She was about to name Scurv, which is a bad idea around here.

"Don't give your life away," she says.

I almost say *For once, I don't want to.*

I walk around the ancient table to the message relay controls.

I should feel more at peace. I've wanted to die for a few good years now, and here I am about to get my wish.

But I've just learned to live. It wasn't three days ago that Jaqi surprised me with . . . something. I don't know what else to call it.

I thought she hated me; apparently she felt tenderly enough toward me to make love. And then sleep. I slept in peace, next to someone I cared for. If that's life, I want it.

Father Rixinius leaves his seat and moves to stand by me, at the control center for their war table, which doubles, of course, as a message center. He doesn't look at me. Of course not.

And we send the hail.

The screen crackles. Here we go. I'm ready to face the big bastard, John Starfire, and get this over with.

And the screen crackles again and I see—

The woman I killed.

Thin face, green eyes narrowed in that calculating way, and lips pursed as she's thinking, and for a few full seconds I swear to God I'm seeing Rashiya, that I didn't actually put my sword through her and take her memories, that somehow the Resistance found a way to bring her back, or to build a template out of her, and . . .

No. Recognition snaps into place with the memories I took from my former lover. Not Rashiya at all. I see these lips moving, begging *Please, I don't want my daughter's body to show up dead on the screens.* I remember—as Rashiya—ignoring the pleas. *You really don't understand what this feels like? I can't stop your father, but we've done all this so you could have a normal life, Rash!*

Stop overreacting, Mom. I can keep my wits.

Rashiya's mother.

She's almost as famous as her husband in her own right; Aranella, the legends went among my crew, was a territorial boss who risked everything to take her division of mixed agricultural and security crosses against their bosses, and steal shipments of food and munitions to create the Resistance. She and her husband John Starfire had a good life, or so the propaganda went, but they had to act to stop injustice.

But that's not how I know Aranella. I know her as a woman divided; she stole and fought and sold her life to the Resistance, but all on the condition that her children would stay out of it. And I know her through the one daughter who defied that. *The Resistance is in my blood, Mom. I'm not going to go the rest of my life knowing that I didn't fight.*

"Aranella?"

She looks long on me, checking every one of my features, following the jigsaw scars across my face.

I wonder if I slurred again, so I open my mouth to ask one more time.

She interrupts. "You're Araskar."

"Yes." I motion toward the tall masked figure behind me. "With Father Rixinius, acting head of the Thuzerian Ruling Council."

Her eyes flicker to Rixinius. "The Order of the Thuzerians is protecting war criminals."

"Those you refer to as war criminals have, for the most part," Father Rixinius says, and I feel his red eye on me, "sought refuge among the Masked Faith, by our code to protect the innocent. They were unjustly forced to work in the dangerous conditions of a hyperdense oxygen mine."

"What gives you the right?"

"The Sanctuary Acts."

Aranella could say a few things here. She could come on strong and say that the Resistance doesn't observe the Sanctuary Acts. They were ratified by the Empire she's just destroyed, after all. Or she could question whether the Thuzerians, a military organization, can claim refugee-right under the Sanctuary Acts.

She won't say any of that.

I know her too well.

"Including him?" She motions to me.

Rixinius looks long on me, red eyes gleaming through the mask. "No," he finally says, "not him." He hastens to add, "Though he distinguished himself greatly by bringing the refugees to the Masked Faith."

Aranella waits a moment longer, never taking her eyes off me. "I know what you are trying to do, Thuzerian. I know who you've taken in here, and I should blast your world to pieces. You are only preserving, lengthening the life of the Empire's injustices."

"Says the people who've brought all the vats back online, and kept the Navy running," I say. The response comes fast. Too fast. Easy, Araskar. Despite the memories, you're not a teenage girl sparring with her mother.

"Who are you protecting, besides this one?" Aranella asks.

Rixinius's eyes flicker toward Paxin, who is standing

out of range of the message, coughing into the stump of her hand. He says, again, "All of them, save this one warrior, qualify under the Sanctuary Acts."

The unspoken offer hangs.

"Very well," Aranella says. "As our first condition of negotiation, I insist on the transfer of this cross, who names himself Araskar, to our custody."

"And your other conditions?" Rixinius asks.

Aranella purses her lips, thinking. The same way she would think when working out a fight between Rashiya and her sisters. "Fifty million in cash, or in a suitable hard-matter equivalent. Water, ore—we can work out the details later. And a pledge of nonaggression against the Resistance."

"In exchange," Rixinius says, "you agree to abide by the Sanctuary Acts in all dealings with the Faith. You will not attempt to reclaim refugees. Other than him."

"It's a good thing you have something I want, monk," Aranella says, looking at me.

"You will abide."

"I will abide. Your little pack of war criminals are safe."

They dither just a bit more. The prisoner and fund exchange will take place at a neutral point beyond the orbit of this planet's moon, in what is technically not native Thuzerian territory. The dreadnoughts will all retreat except one.

This time tomorrow, I'll be in Aranella's hands.

Another of Rashiya's memories surfaces. One of their endless fights about her joining the Resistance. *I would never forgive myself if you fell in battle. I would never forgive you, never forgive your father.*

Mom, Rashiya said, angry to be having this discussion yet again, *we would be the wrong people to hate. Just find the person who killed me and throw them out an airlock.*

I go to the window, stare out at the planet. It's raining. Sheeting cold gray drops. It's winter here. The curtains of rain sweep off the sea, batter the huts of the refugee camp.

Living sounded so good.

3

Jaqi

IN THE DARKNESS, all I hear is our breathing.

Quiet. Sometimes I like the quiet, but too often it reminds me of space—of the feeling that if it's too quiet, and too cold, you might have lost atmos. I think of that one moment I was out in the killing vacuum, the moisture in my body instantly freezing. So I twist around in the sheets, next to Araskar, press up against him, just to make a little noise.

Araskar shifts a bit against the pillow too. The running lights of the ship flicker outside, shine through the window onto his face. Plenty of ridges over the face, the imperfect scars where he's been pieced back together.

I touch the scars that jigsaw across what was the bridge of his nose. "This why you chose your name?" I ask. "Araskar?"

"Ha, no," he says. Under the covers, his hand rests on my belly. A rough hand, with all them calluses from swordfighting, but still feels nice on my soft belly. "Not at all. I was with my friend Barathuin, and we were supposed to pick names, because vat-cooked crosses didn't get real names, you know. So we'd go through these old record books with Jorian names, the real ones. Barathuin's name was some warrior-king, something glorious, and mine ... I think it was on a list of minor officials. I just liked the way it sounded."

"That fella still with the Resistance?" I ask him. "Barathuin?"

"No," Araskar says. "No, he's dead. They're all dead. My entire vat-batch, my entire first battalion."

"Right. I remember now. You said that, on Trace."

"They all died the moment we hit our first Imperial ship. Rashiya, the girl I killed on Trace, was the last of my battalion. The only survivor, besides me."

"That's why it was so hard to face up?"

He doesn't speak, just grunts a little assent.

"What do you suppose we'll do when this is over?" I ask him. I said something like this before, back before we fell into bed.

"Told you, I don't place too much stock in the future."

"I heard you, slab, but I en't talking philosophically. Just want to know what you might do if old John Starfire kicked it tomorrow. Come on now, you got any plans?"

He exhales. "Play guitar. Learn how to play it right. I only know two chords so far."

"That's a good start, slab. Where is your guitar?"

"The guitar you gave me is still back on the moon of Trace. Thought it would be safer in the desert than on Shadow Sun Seven. I guess I'll go back there and see the sights again. Then I'll come back—here, I suppose? Here, and I'll see if there's a Thuzerian who's sworn to fight evil and stay celibate and teach guitar." He breathes into my hair. "You?"

"Oh, I thought about it plenty. I'm going to go see some plays, visit some museums, do the stuff real folk talk about."

"Real folk. We're real folk now, aren't we?"

"Depends who you ask, I suppose. Crosses have got to be as real as any other sentient, now."

"We're real," he says. "And we're—"

And that's where the memory slips away. Araskar's face blurs. The only part left of his face is the scars, now, an empty field of brown skin with scars dotting it, but no eyes, no nose, no mouth.

He speaks, but I don't recognize the words.

I think I been dragged somewhere. I reckon I been hurt. Everything else is fragments. My memories break into shards and bounce around my head. Faces blur and names and I don't reckon I remember a thing and this fella who done stabbed me—who is he?—still talking.

"You don't get it."

Am I back with Araskar? This fella got scars. Hard to tell. Araskar had a lot of scars, though I remember him lying next to me, saying things about them after we had slack. But I can't see his face. Only the scars.

"You killing me?" Why would Araskar kill me? Thought we was getting along real well. We did—a thing.

Can't recall what it was.

"Ha." He actually puts something cool on my leg, where he cut me, and another on my arm, where the other cut was. Synthskin gel-packs. Kind of thing crosses use in a battle. Kind of thing heals you, helps you keep fighting till you can get properly stitched. What's this? "I need to know why it speaks to you."

"It . . ."

"You felt it, when you came in. The pure-space being." He, whoever he is, presses another gel-pack to my shoulder. My shoulder, I'm fairly sure. Not anyone else's. "When did you first hear its voice? When you ran to that Suit mainframe? Before that?"

"It."

"You know, I wanted to believe you too." His voice softens. "I thought perhaps I wasn't chosen, wasn't fated, and for just a moment, it was a relief. A relief to stop doubting, to stop being afraid." And then his voice rises again, like some kind of preacher. "Then I remembered how it felt. How the words burned inside me. Do you know what it's like to speak, and know that the will of the Starfire itself is speaking through you?"

"I . . ." My mouth is dry. No, this en't Araskar. Maybe this is Z, his dour face locked in anger, muttering to himself. Something about blood and honor, I'd guess.

"I've been hunting this place for years. All that trouble to get one memory crypt from Formoz, and you find it first." He leans closer. "You know why the Shir don't come here?"

"Don't name the devil," I say.

"Devil is more apt than you know. They are fallen, like the devils of old Earth myth. They almost remember what they were."

He sounds like Z, being all cryptic. "Blood and honor," I say to him, hoping he'll respond and turn out to be Z.

"What's that?"

"Blood and honor. You . . ." No wait, this en't Z. I en't even sure I remember Z. My memory done broke. He's . . .

He's my enemy. And he's gonna kill me like this, rip me to bits.

I gotta get out of here.

He's sheathed his sword in order to slap the gel-packs on me. He turns around. Touches something at the controls. "Why won't you talk to me?" he mutters. "What did she do to bring you close?"

Okay. I got enough sense in my woozy head to see a way out of here. Just gotta kill this fella. My enemy. I know he's my enemy. I can remember that.

It's simple, self. Grab that sword. Pull it out of the sheath and stick him with it.

Simple. Except it's so hard to move.

I start to move, and blood runs down my arms and legs. Them synthskin packs haven't had time to meld with my flesh. My wounds are raw and ragged.

"Bend, pull..." He mutters a thing. A thing I recognize. A song my mother used to sing. He sings it, only half in tune. "Bend, pull, break your back..."

The cadences, the rhythm of the song is all mine. My mother's.

What did she look like? I should be able to remember her face—that thing had her face, a minute ago.

And I realize I can't recall my mother's face.

He took that from me.

Now that pisses me off, and strength rushes through me, the strength born of anger, and I get to my feet, ignoring the pain and the blood.

He's closed his eyes, focusing on the song, which is how I close the distance before he whips the sword out, and I'm too close, and by some miracle, I get my hands on his sword and yank, but he's got a death grip on the blade—and I knee him in the thigh, and he must have a wound there because he folds, falls backward—and I get the sword turned, even with his grip still on it—

I stab. He twists.

The sword just connects, tearing through his body armor and into the flesh of his side, below his ribs.

I stab John Starfire, just enough. And blood drips down my arm, wound breaking open, and white fire lashes up when it reaches the blade. And I—

I suck up his memories like I'm a thirsty girl who just found a cache of good water.

The jelly is wet, and sticky. The darkness is pleasant, the light hurts, but somehow he knows he must open his eyes.

Eyes. They are called eyes. He will see with them.

He knows things. He hadn't known them, and now they are filling his head, one after another, like musical notes crowded on top of one another.

The fear in his eyes is the same fear come rushing into me through this sword. And I'm being born from a vat, in the memory I steal.

Music. He understands music. He had not, a moment ago, but now he has a corpus of the best music in his head, symphonic and rollicking, fuzzy electric and echoing acoustic, all the best music from a thousand years of empire.

Empire. He understands that.

The Empire he overthrew. *I* overthrew.

Jaqi and John Starfire braid together.

He is a cross. There have to be crosses, because someone has to fight the war, because there are millions of them out there, and they will eat suns and planets without the crosses to man the ships and the planet-crackers and the battles.

And thus the Empire can have peace.

There must be crosses.

Crosses must fight and die.

He twists and with a spray of blood, falls away from the sword.

I face him.

"I en't you," he says, sounding a lot like me.

"Not yourself either," I say, and I sound just like him.

He gets to his feet, shaking, and faster than he should be able to, he leaps on me and grabs the sword away. He faces me, holding up the blade—and crumples, clutching the wound in his side.

But I can't fight back. His memories en't like the ones I took before. They feel alive inside me, twisting through me. They hurt.

"What did you take?" He gasps out the words. Drops to his knees, grabs synthskin packs, slaps them on his wound.

I en't sure if it's Jaqi or John Starfire talking, but I need to get away.

I run.

I'm remembering a thing, and remembering it is vicious, like living through every hot, angry minute I ever felt. I'm remembering his first battle in the Dark Zone. Where he jumped ship.

One minute he is rushing from one side of the medical bay to the other, plasma packs in one hand, a thermo-regulator in the other, preparing for the influx of the wounded—the next minute the wall of the medical bay is gone, open to the Dark Zone.

The gravity generator shifts, turns up to heavy gravity to lock them to the floor. Something goes wrong—he slides, and vacuum.

Cold. Exploding pain in his ears. He remembers his training and presses the sense-field.

The field, and the oxygen, pop into existence around him. His lungs throb with pain as he breathes in the sweet oxygen. Bright shards flash red across space. Sickly white-blue light springs out of nowhere, danced in patterns, and tears everything apart.

And then the ship comes apart.

And he sees them.

So huge, so dark, lit by the half-light. Enough to see planet-sized faces with spars of teeth, the immense bellies where stars burn.

Their voices are like breaking glass. <u>Little things made to die. Little things made for us to eat. Nameless little ones.</u>

With that memory, of seeing the devil, music rushes into me.

I run into the hall, and immediately regret it. I have to go. I have to go somewhere—back to the ship, back to safety, where I can figure out who I am. "Are you there?" I say to the Starfire itself.

That music cascades through me.

"I gotta get out of here!"

My memories—no, *his* memories—but they are mine too—they twist, they core me out. *The cold almost has him. The sense-field has lost its air, so much of it already passed through his lungs. He scuttles across the surface of the ship he's found, numb woodblock hands failing to find a port, an entrance that can be opened, anything—*

The moisture in his eyes is freezing. His ears burn and ring. The cold of space will take him, like it has taken his entire ship, all his batch-mates, everyone he cares about—

He presses his hand against something like a sensor—and an airlock opens.

The music rushes into me. "Get me out of here," I say as I slump to the ground, bloody. "Get me somewhere safe."

And just like that, the music answers and a node opens up around me.

4

Araskar

IT'S A CRAPPY DAY to go for a hike, but it's my last day planetside, so I'll be damned if I'm spending it indoors. Rain lashes us. My clothes are wet through despite the slicker. Rain patters off the metal roofs of the hastily constructed shelters all around us. Mud runs in thick rivers along the streets of the refugee camp. The refugees of Shadow Sun Seven, formerly the elite of the galaxy, huddle inside their shelters and thank God for a roof. Paxin walks next to me, clad in an equally soaked slicker. We hike slowly, up the hill, toward the air hangar that is the only part of the refugee camp that predates the refugees.

The painting's back on side of the hangar.

I step slowly and carefully up a rapidly eroding hill of mud. Close enough to the picture to stop and stare.

In the picture, Saint Jaqi stares out at the universe, her dark skin reflecting the light of a surrounding circle of stars.

"Rixinius has had this painted over twice already,"

Paxin says. "Actually, this one's kind of a rush job. Last one was better. That's not what her nose looks like at all. And they need to learn to draw hands." She's wearing her temporary prosthetic hands today. She points with her prosthetic finger, a thing of spindly metal.

The fresh paint is not quite dry; bits of Jaqi run in the rain. But not her eyes. Her painted dark eyes. I can't help it—it hits me. Just the same way it's hit these refugees.

It really is like looking on God.

Or the Starfire.

It's not what her face looks like. She never has that beatific, wise look the painter's given her—most of the time she just looks hungry and curious.

But I look at this, and I realize I've seen it. I've seen her do genuine miracles. Me, who was supposed to die in the Dark Zone, who should have died a thousand times since, in our first assault or on Irithessa or when I was chasing Jaqi. Instead, I've lived long enough to see miracles.

Realizing that—you also realize how amazing this day is. Sheeting rain and mud and all. Gray skies over stormy sea. People, human and otherwise, running around the refugee camp to stay out of the rain.

Everything I've been through, all of it, was all for a day like today.

I can't help laughing.

"You okay?" Paxin asks.

I might be. "If you write about this at all . . . don't fake it. Tell the truth about who we were." I don't even mean Jaqi, I realize. I turn and fix her with my gaze. "Tell the truth about me."

"I'd be happy to." Paxin's face softens. "But I still believe you'll get through this."

Hope. It's a worse temptation than any drug.

"This is wrong," says Adept Alsethus.

I've only met this woman once before. She captains the dreadnought that took on the refugees, and when I met her before I'd been up for hours, and was half burnt and near frozen from splitting Shadow Sun Seven in half.

She was angry then and is angry now.

Consistent.

I've been on a lot of shitty little shuttles lately. The Thuzerian shuttle, christened *Sword of Faith 529*, is rather luxurious. It's meant to hold an elite team of Adepts, and that's who accompanies me—all of them are big burly sentients who look like they've spent the week in the gym.

"This is not what the servants of God should do."

I don't bother with that. Instead, I motion to the huge people around us. "I sure could have used this group when we were breaking into Shadow Sun Seven last week."

"You came protecting a group of refugees, and we give you up to save them." She interlocks her four arms in a way I've never seen before, but I'm guessing it's a bit like a human shaking their head in disgust. "What have we become? I heard what happened in the Council chamber. I heard how the leader of the refugees came to defend you, and Father Rixinius instead offered you to the Resistance. Where is our faith? The Council will find an uprising of their own if they're not careful."

"Easy," I say. "Infighting only helps the Resistance. I offered myself."

"Yourself?" Her eyes narrow, and two of her arms cross over the enormous sword emblazoned on her tabard. "This was your idea? Do you want to die?"

"I used to." I hardly realize I've said it. It's weird to be so honest about something. Especially with one of these religious types who place such stock in honesty. "I think life might be worth living now."

"Of course it is. Life is a gift. Each moment is given us by God, in His mercy."

Religious types seem to forget that not everyone comes to life the way they do. "In my case, life was given by the Empire."

"All sentient life is given by God. And do not say a

word about crosses and sentience. I have always believed crosses to be sentient. None of us believed the Empire's propaganda. This galaxy was built on the blood of crosses. It is a thousand-year-sin."

"Thanks," I say. Her words could have come straight out of one of John Starfire's speeches, but I don't mention that. The ironies are piled high around here. Almost like every revolutionary is destined to be a despot, and every addict who finds hope is destined to die.

Shit, I'm maudlin.

She hits the bulkhead. "You know, if this broke, all the time I've had—all the beauty I've seen, all I've loved, all the worlds I've stood on—they would mean nothing against the cold."

"Are you trying to convert me still?"

"With so much darkness, you must choose light. Faith is a choice, Araskar. You choose to believe because the alternative is despair."

"Oh, there is something greater than all sentience out there," I say. "The problem is, it lives in the Dark Zone."

"Don't mock."

"I don't."

I can tell she wants to say more. Her sort wants to save my sort. That's the way the universe is made.

"Don't worry about me," I tell Alsethus. "I know death well by now."

"Any fool can see you want to live. I don't need God to tell me that."

I can't respond. Something stuck in my gullet.

And then she yells. "Shields!"

"Shield are up—" says one of the pilots—and then our shuttle rocks with the impact of shards against our sense-fields.

Bright red shards spin in a thousand patterns through space around us. From the dreadnoughts and the gunships—Resistance fighters blazing away, every weapon they have—

The ship topples, and this time spins—we must have been hit by a heavy-load shot—we're free-floating now, gravity gone—and it doesn't matter for a moment, because for a moment I think this is it, we're dead—

The ship rights itself. "Return fire!" Alsethus orders. "And strap in!"

"What the hell?" No one hears me say it, but I can't fathom this. I *know* Aranella. Know her through Rashiya's memories. She isn't the type to shoot the messenger. I grab a chair and pull myself down, strap in as the jerks of battle replace artificial gravity.

We send a barrage back. Gunships close with us now, a swarm of them having erupted from the Resistance dreadnoughts. From three of the five dreadnoughts. Two are still holding fire. Behind the gunships, smaller brown shapes—Moths, the individual insectoid fighters.

The shuttle takes another hit, and Adept Alsethus bellows more orders, and we go into a dive, circle, spin, dodging the clouds of shards that keep coming our way.

Heavier shards fill space around us as the Thuzerian dreadnoughts fire back. Gleaming points of red streak across space, tear through the gunships and scatter against the heavy shields of the Resistance dreadnoughts. By the buzz on our intercom, more battle shuttles are entering the fray.

Our ship rights itself—and another shard lands, rocking us back and forth. "Go to battle mode," Alsethus commands. It gets colder as environmental controls minimize.

Alsethus and her gunners yell orders back and forth. We spin around and fire at two gunships, taking them by surprise. A half-dozen Moths swarm us, spitting shards. Our ship rocks and spins and the thrusters blow all over the ship, pinging warning signs as they try to arrest our velocity to keep us from being crushed.

Thrust five times Imperial gravity replaces the art-grav, and then the thrusters catch us, make a stomach-twisting return to zero. Then another spin and more G-forces. Several Thuzerians hitch up their masks and puke. My cross engineering holds and so does my stomach.

"The sense-fields can't take any more of this pummeling," the lead pilot says. "We need to return to the dreadnought."

"As long as we can dodge their shards long enough," Alsethus says through gritted teeth.

That's when I see it. "No!" I say. "Turn!"

"What are you talking about, Araskar?"

"Turn and attack. That's a planet-cracker."

Right there on the sensors, although you'd have to know what you're looking at. Right off our bow, a swarm of Moths is guarding a large white shape.

Alsethus magnifies it on the viewscreen. It looks like a fat missile. In truth, from a better angle, we would see that the "missile" shell is only a half circle, over a shard big enough to survive entry into a planet's atmosphere, big enough to withstand hits from orbital defense. Once there, the giant shard will tear through the planet's crust, sending up a billowing cloud of dust that blacks out the sky and triggers a supervolcanic eruption, to make the planet completely uninhabitable.

You can kill any planet with any decent-sized asteroid, but orbital defense platforms blow those up; firing shards at a planet-cracker will just increase its volatility.

"We won't be able to stop it from just here," Alsethus says. She gets on the private intercom to her bosses; after a moment her face turns sour. "Head for the planet-cracker and suit up."

"What is it?" I ask.

"Our instructions are to fly as close as we can, then suit up and stop it manually. Firing at it will, at best, make it blow early. Hopefully the planet will only catch a few fragments."

"The only way to stop it manually is to ride it out," I say. "Those things don't have much in the way of navigation—you have to reprogram and to stay with it until it's hit the new target." For a moment, in the shaking, rattling ship, Alsethus and I both stare at each other, thinking the same thing. "The Resistance fleet."

"We've got to land on the planet-cracker and reprogram it to hit the Resistance," Alsethus shouts.

When she says it, it sounds even crazier than when I do.

"Last chance, Araskar," she asks me. "Would you like to pledge yourself to God and the Saints before death? We do not have time for a full rite, but God will understand."

"Ask me later," I say, unbuckling to float toward the spacesuits, then clutching a handhold to keep from being thrown into the wall as the ship rattles again.

"By then it will be too late," she says.

5

Jaqi

A BARE, BLEEDING BODY in pure space. I should be torn to bits by the journey, but something lifts me up and carries me into the cold.

And John Starfire's memory rips through me.

Formoz of Keil has a kindly face. Most of them do, these bluebloods who find a conscience. A kindly, soft face, possibly a little windburnt from parasailing on private lakes and beachfront property.

"You have this in writing," Aranella says.

Formoz holds it up. "Emperor Turka has agreed to abdicate in favor of a provisional government. I told you, we were at negotiating stage. A coalition is the next stage—and then, recognition of sentience. We're so close."

Jaceren, who still struggles to think of himself as John Starfire, realizes he's clenching his sword hilt. He's grown so used to the feel of it. To the security of a weapon at his waist.

It is a strange feeling, to accept that you will never stop wearing a weapon. Even in peace.

"You'll just have to wait." Formoz wants to sound reassuring. "I know there's no romance in waiting. But give it time. Democracy is slow. Every faction in the provisional government has agreed to ban custom engineering of soldiers, and to treat the Resistance as a valid political party." He shifts. "In the meantime, John, I will send over that memory crypt I told you about, as soon as I get coded coordinates."

"Coordinates coming your way."

"Next relay opening is tomorrow," Formoz says. "I'll get you an update then."

The hologram goes dark, as does John and Aranella's quarters.

"I thought so," Aranella says. "Do you think he knows about the assault?"

"Yes. He thinks we won't attack now." His words are loud as the thunder of shards in atmos. "Today."

"Today." Her breathing is a heavy sound in the dark room.

"He's right that it moves slow." He focuses on how the sword hilt feels in his hand; clenched tight, it becomes a part of him, like a longer arm. "That's why the sentients of the Empire forget so easily." The other words come to his lips so easily. The words feel good, right. "I spent one hour in hard vacuum, watching a Shir kill a million crosses with my naked eyes. A short time in a man's life, even if he is a vat-born cross. That short time changed me. Show me killing Emperor Turka on every screen in the galaxy, and they'll remember."

And then I open my eyes and see the black of space above me.

Oh, shit, am I in vacuum?

No, there's atmos.

It's cold and thin, and smells all funny, and I suspect there's a leak somewhere, but I'm breathing atmos.

And space is up there.

But overlaying the stars, sense-field points shimmer. Some kind of relay. Points in the sky that flash bits of overlapping fields between them to keep in an atmosphere. Like a lattice. A kind of Jorian miracle I've seen before, where different fixed generators all talk to each other from their spot in the sky and keep the sense-field running.

I can't quite move yet, but I cast my eyes around. I'm on a street, stone all broken up and corroded by years of atmos.

I manage to get up on my elbows and see the kind of place I only ever dreamed about.

It's one of them Jorian cities, like I've seen on pictures from Irithessa. Big old crystal pyramids in the distance. Fluted columns marching along the streets, and a strange sort of trees I en't never seen before—trees that shimmer bluish-green, twisting as if in some wind I can't feel. Some of the towers even stretch up beyond the crystal network in the sky, and I figure them for node-relay towers. Palaces in the distance too, all domes and towers. Stretching all the way up to the relay's lights. Some of them go above the relay, apparently meant to have landing platforms.

It's bigger and fancier than anything I ever imagined.

I remember Irithessa—I remember smoke drifting between crystal pyramids and huge node-relay towers—from the memories I got from John Starfire.

This is fancier.

Gravity's real low here—or so I think at first. I stand up and walk, and I have to be at half-Imperial. The next step, though, feels about Imperial standard. Grav en't low, then—the grav generator is going out.

It means they once had lots of intersecting generating fields, but some fields have failed while some others are still working. Some of my steps carry me what ten steps would in normal grav—and then a second later, I come down hard in standard Imperial gravity. Huh.

Walking will be fun around here.

At the end of one of the streets, not too far from me, the lattice lights come down to the planet's surface. Beyond the lights, there's the gray of an airless surface, and beyond that, I think, another dome covered with more twinkling lights over another shimmering city.

A full city? Here? I know them Jorians was supposed to be wise, but what kind of fool builds a city under a dome on an airless moon what can't be terraformed? I'd bet my left ass cheek this moon en't got a magnetic field worth a shit in space. Why not leave it alone? Hell, there's plenty of ecosphere templates left over that can be filled and set to orbiting, and then all a body needs is the mining station.

Who made this place?

It doesn't have the marks of an Imperial reconstruction—a fake designed to give legitimacy to the Second Empire's regime. Instead it—Wait, those en't my thoughts. I stand there and shake my head. "I en't John Starfire. I'm Jaqi the scab."

Weird how it feels to have to say that.

Hang on. Them stars.

I blink, not sure if I'm hallucinating from the pain where John Starfire stabbed me. But I made it my business to know stars, seeing as how I can't read words. I can recognize just about any place in the galaxy by the orientation of stars.

Not now, though.

These stars are strange.

Can't find the Dark Zone. Can't find what folks call the Field of Fire, the dense spread of stars at the galactic core. There's a smear of stars that could be a galactic core, but it en't *my* galactic core.

I en't never seen this configuration of stars before.

This en't my galaxy.

I force myself up, despite the pain. The synthskin gel-packs are doing their work, but not enough. Warm blood is still trickling into my clothes, and the cuts all opened again when I ran.

Up above, a flash, and the whole network of lattice-lights overhead flashes, like light traveling along a web. So not just any airless planet—one prone to meteor strikes. I stumble around, on my feet, and as my view shifts I see it—a blue planet beyond this empty city. I must be standing on that planet's moon. And right now, it looks lovely down there. Blue oceans and brown-green land and swirls of cloud.

Something about it strikes me, on the deep insides. I feel like I used to when I'd spin out of pure space to Bill's, like I've come home.

After a moment, I speak. "Why didn't folk live on that nice planet instead of up here on this dead moon?"

I keep walking. It's cold in here, and the air is thin; my lungs are starting to hurt. At least the trees smell nice. I reckon they're some kind of air recycler. Might be I'm far from the oxygen works and if I get there, I can find some stronger air. Might be there's someone still alive here, or an automated ferry system, could take me down to that nice planet below, or better yet, a ship that could get me there.

I walk and I try not to think about what I just did. I come through a node. Unprotected. Should have torn me apart.

To what is, far as I can tell, the far side of the universe.

That don't matter now. Need to find a weapon. I'm still limping, but the bleeding has slowed now. If I came through a node, I can go back, and I want to be armed when I do.

So. Weapons. And bandages wouldn't hurt, to help the synthskin do its thing.

I think on weapons for a moment, hoping that one of John Starfire's memories will pop up and teach me how to swing a sword.

Nothing.

Aw hell, could have used something like that.

I try a door to one of them crystal buildings. Nothing. I try going up some stairs, along the outside apex of a pyramid. I climb the stairs halfway up the pyramid, bouncing through low grav, until I hit a particular patch of Imperial grav, and falling suddenly seems a danger, and then I go back down the stairs real quick. Heights are only nice when there en't no grav to go with them.

Everything's like a massive monument to ghosts. This one pyramid, what I got part of the way up, is almost bigger than that node-tower on the moon of Trace. The node-towers stretching up beyond the sense-field, further into the city, would dwarf any structure I ever seen.

I get back down to the stone of the street, broken up in some spots by tree roots.

Along the street a bit farther, there are some less fancy buildings, what look like storefronts. Their roofs are still fancy slanting crystal, of that super-hard light structure the Jorians built with, but these look like the sorts of the places folk might live. It looks like there may have been a private sense-field here one time, but now it's gone, so I slip in.

Inside, everything covered in dust. Whatever food-stuffs was in here have long ago rotted away. A door at the back, keyed half open. A funny smell in here, like the dust is made of . . .

"Oh."

I cross into the back, and there's a small living space. The bare plasticene frame of a couch, long gone moldy and black, possibly because of the consequences of two people dying on it.

There are two skeletons huddled against each other on the couch.

This is no good. Something killed these folk, but it weren't the devil. I turn and run right out of there. Dead folk in an ecosphere—that's a sure sign of something bad going down, a sure sign you need to run.

But once I'm out, I realize there was a cupboard in

there, and they might have had some weapons or bandages. I take a breath. "Easy, spaceways girl. Check for medical supplies."

I force myself to go back in. It en't easy.

The smells in here are of rot that's turned to dust in the last thousand years. They must have built a nice air system, to keep this place in atmos this long. The only way there's still atmos here is if they have self-regulating reverse-cells, kind of thing cost Bill near a year's pay.

I go through the cupboards. Find something that might have been bandages once, but they crumbled to bits ages ago. Oxygen'll do that. I exhale heavily, and then think about how I'm breathing the stuff of dead folk and get the hell out of there.

I go through the back doorway, into an alleyway behind the house. Lots more doors here. Lots more houses.

Lots more of the dead.

In the spaceways, we was suspicious because it was good practice. Everyone dead on a spaceship or ecosphere meant get the hell away. Even if they look a few hundred years gone.

This tests my nerves worse than fighting John Starfire. I get into a few more houses. More skeletons, most of them human, though in one there's a desiccated cricket corpse, a hollow exoskeleton that crumbles away soon as I shift the air. Whatever killed these folk, it took everyone.

The virus the humans made. Somewhere on the other side of the galaxy there will be whole planets full of the dead.

The memory bubbles up and then is gone.

"I reckon you make sense, stolen memory," I say, to kill the silence. This is the sort of thing happens when a supervirus, like what them Matakas used at a time, gets into a sealed ecosphere.

Which means I been exposed to this virus. But as I figure the whole place is a thousand years dead at least, maybe—please, gods and goshes—the virus gone inert.

Or maybe—another memory pops up. *Crosses would have to be resistant to the virus. They knew what we must be.* The memory floats across my mind, and then vanishes. Hm.

I sit in an alley outside another house of the dead, thinking that it would be nice to find some vacuum-sealed bandages, and maybe a gun—and then I see movement.

Who is that? Someone just walked by on the street. Reckon there's people here after all?

I sneak to the end of the alley I'm in, peer out at the main street, trying to ignore the pain in my arm.

John Starfire is walking down the street, away from me, clutching his side.

Hell! How did he get here?

He must have heard something. He turns around, looks up and down the street, and speaks as if he knows I can hear him. "This was a mixed-use district, looks like. Anything worth keeping would have been in the warehousing districts a mile north."

Okay, maybe he don't know I can hear him now, if he been saying that.

"You like this? This was the humans' handiwork, girl. They created the virus to kill Jorians. Worked, but killed its share of humans too." He turns around. I feel like he must hear my breathing, it comes so fast. "This is all that remains of the First Empire. Earth, up there, is just as dead."

That's Earth? That fine little planet is Earth lost?

I been shipped back to the home of humanity?

I start edging down the hallway. I reckon that if we're in a sealed dome—sort of like an ecosphere, maybe before ecosphere were a thing—there's got to be control stations, places where I can figure on how to find weapons, something to kill this bastard. And maybe some guidance for how I done put myself here.

Then he answers that thought. "I didn't think it could be done until I saw it. You reached out to the pure Starfire, and you made a new node, spinning right back here to the birthplace of the disease." He pauses. "Don't you understand? Will you keep running, or face me?"

I say it just loud enough that I feel the words in my mouth, but they don't make no noise. "No more running."

I mean it. If that's really Earth what was lost, then I've run about as far as anyone can run. For all his bluster, he's as much a stranger here as I am. And there en't no one like a spaceways scab for scavenging up weapons.

Only one Chosen One is coming out of this place.

6

Araskar

OUR SHUTTLE CAREENS TOWARD the planet-cracker. Inside, suited up, we shake as the vessel takes hit after hit. Atmos streams out of the shuttle. Alsethus leans hard on the thrusters to slow us down enough for an attack.

The planet-cracker has enough of a sense-field to prevent it from taking serious shard-hits.

I look at the poor Resistance bastards in their spacesuits, clinging to a planet-cracker as it falls toward a planetful of refugees, and I mentally count all the ways that John Starfire is violating his own dictums. *We are sentients, and we should not exist only to die.* Here's forty sentients, custom-made to die. *The vats must be stopped, and those who came out of the vats must be treated with value.*

"Forty of them." Alsethus's voice interrupts John Starfire's in my head. "Twelve of us. What do we have that they do not?"

"We have faith!" the shouts ring in the intercom.

"We have faith." Alsethus again. "Araskar, you will have

to lead us. You know their tactics."

"I lead?" I squeak. Of course. It's not a bad tactic, to put the experienced one in charge—if you're the sort of idiot that goes by faith. "Uh, well, these will all be fresh from the vat, but don't mistake them for inexperienced. They've had a standard Imperial data dump, and their muscles are conditioned. Don't waste time with anything fancy, because they won't—they'll just go for killing blows."

"We'll drop inside the sense-field, yes?" Alsethus asks.

"Drop in, get through the shock. Don't use shards unless you have no doubt that you'll hit your target. Vat-cooked soldiers have the reflexes of longtime fighters, but they're untested. They'll be more cautious about shooting."

"We have faith!" Again the shout. "God bears our wounds! God carries our standard! In the darkest of vacuum, God is our node!"

How can I follow that? "Let's shoot something."

The shuttle bay doors open—

Shard-fire roars into here and everything explodes and we go flying into space. I manage to orient myself enough to lay fire across the surface of the planet-cracker, but I can't see the results—I can only work my thrusters, trying to correct the force that launched me into the vacuum.

I spin through space. It's suddenly silent, except for the hiss of the intercom in my ear. Shards, wreckage, shredded bodies—all fly past me. Most humanoid sentients would be disoriented, but I was built to home in on a military target, built to keep my head under heavy thrust and g-forces, and every time the planet-cracker comes into view, I orient myself, push my suit's thrusters.

I hit the planet-cracker's protective sense-field, and my intercom screeches in my ear as the field interferes with it. This is a heavy-duty field, powered off the massive shard, and it rattles the insides of my teeth. It's made specifically to repel shards, a frequency that breaks the integrity of unthunium, but it's a frequency that rattles a sentient's bodily integrity too.

My head splitting and my body screaming, I land on the edge of the planet-cracker. My magnetic boots gain traction, suctioning to the metal, and I look up to see a storm of Resistance troops charging me, swords in hand.

I fire a few pithy shards at the closest ones, blowing them apart. Their blood and guts fly off into space, freezing into chunks of rock-hard flesh that'll fly through vacuum forever.

I can't risk too many shards or I might punch through and hit the enormous planet-cracking shard beneath the metal shell. Blow it now and it'll take the Thuzerian ships in range. So I holster my shard-blaster.

"Alsethus?" I say into the intercom.

There's no answer as one vat-cooked soldier comes toward me, and I catch his thrust and our blades spring together, and apart.

He's using some basic moves, stabbing and stabbing again, the kind that kill quickly and avoid anything fancy, but he hasn't trained enough for vacuum—with no gravity, he carries himself forward too far, and his lunges are too vicious, too easy for me to sidestep.

I slash open his spacesuit under his arm, letting space into his lungs.

As he dies, I catch a glimpse of panicked eyes through that visor.

Born to die. Hasn't done a thing in a few weeks of life that didn't lead to this. And yet so afraid.

"Open channel," I say to the intercom, as another lunges at me, and I scramble back. This bastard has trained for zero, and her moves are too fast. I stumble backward, and suddenly there's nothing under me, and I fall back against the nothingness of space and I have to activate my thrusters; then I'm back in her face and our blades close fast, too fast.

It's only dumb luck that my opponent's blade slides past my side while mine finds a home, jabbing under the helmet. The poor stupid idiot stumbles back, blood filling her helmet. She actually unhooks the helmet, some remnant of an old and dumb survival mechanism winning over all the cross conditioning.

She's got Joskiya's face. A face I know well, a face a lot of my slugs had. Vacuum freezes the blood that has soaked her hair and her face, and she stares at me, empty-eyed. As dead as all my friends who bore her face. I can't help it—I stop and stare.

"Araskar!" The Thuzerians yell in the intercom. Some of them made the landing on the planet-cracker—black, heavy soulswords light up by the light of the red shards flying overhead.

"Report," I say, as I begin running along the edge of the planet-cracker.

Seven of the twelve soldiers sound off. I hear Alsethus's strained voice. Still with us.

"Whoever's closest to the front of this thing, meet me there." I run along the edge of the metal. The planet-cracker is basically a massive half-dome, protecting the shard underneath, and moving faster and faster on just a few small thrusters. Even through the suit, I feel the heat of the shard from underneath the side.

Something punches my leg. A shard? No—it's an actual projectile weapon, just a rod of metal that's been sharpened and launched. I hardly feel it, as that leg is entirely artificial after Shadow Sun Seven, but I do feel the suit losing atmos. More little metal fragments go flying through the air.

Smart. Crosses get a data dump that teaches us how to make basic weapons, including crossbows, and the danger of shards on this planet-cracker means they would, of course, resort to simpler weapons. Thuzerian groans and shouts come through my comm as they each meet a sharpened steel rod. Another one sinks into my arm. That one actually hurts, finds some flesh, unlike my leg, which is mostly synthskin and steel rods.

I turn and fire shards, damning caution, hit two nearby Resistance soldiers who are halfway through reloading their improvised crossbows. Blood soaks the inside of my suit. I'm colder. The suit should seal itself around the puncture, but it won't be perfect; I'll lose atmos the longer I stay out here.

Not that I was planning on going back.

That makes me think of Jaqi, and I wonder if she'll make it back.

I can't think of her now. I'll think of her when I'm sure I'll die. Not now.

I run until I reach the front of the planet-cracker. There's a Thuzerian there, holding off two sword-wielding Resistance fighters. One reaches for a pocket crossbow, locked to his leg. I leap across the distance, run him through, switch my stance, and both me and the Thuzerian soldier stab the other soldier, then toss his body off the surface into space.

"There's only a basic guidance system," I say, as I drop to my knees. My knees magnetize automatically to the surface.

"They've wounded me," the Thuzerian's voice hisses in the intercom, and I recognize Alsethus. "My lungs." Her voice garbles.

"Stay with me," I say. "I need—aw hell." The guidance system is protected up here. I can hotwire it, but I would have to get underneath it.

Down there, under the shield, with the big, planet-cracking shard.

"Tether me," I say. It'll be too hot down there for my boots to keep purchase. She nods, and attaches the tether to herself.

"I promise you can give me your rites when I get back up here," I say.

She raises a hand in a universal sign of approval.

I'm guessing that her lungs are filling with blood, or the equivalent for her species. Another one dead.

And me still not dead yet.

She turns to face the Resistance troops, wielding two swords and shields between her four arms, and I go out and around the nose of the planet-cracker. There is little to the front of it—a half circle, wide and hot even through my suit, this close to the shard.

I swing out from under it, and immediately my spacesuit protests, temperature alarms ringing as we get within vicinity of the planet-cracking shard.

An enormous, glaring red lump of unthunium, the size of a small shuttle, stares back at me like a Shir's eye. Could mistake it for a very angry meteor if you met it on the spaceways.

This is a major Imperial planet-cracker. Despite the name, it's really made to kill an adult Shir.

Being so close to it, my suit is overheating. The suit is already broken down from the projectiles that have pierced it, and it's typically meant to keep a person warm, not cool them off. Not to mention the radiation shielding is only meant for standard radiation encountered in space. Crosses have a heavy tolerance to most radiation. We can handle amounts that would poison other sentients. But no one should be this close to this much unthunium.

Which is to say, suddenly I'm hot.

It's all right, though, because I find the guidance system. Right above me, tucked into the crook between the shard and the half circle nose. I scramble up, my suit beeping alarms in my ear, and pull a couple of wires, disconnect the brain of the planet-cracker. The thrusters will stop, but they are only for course corrections anyway; it's still on target. I need to reconnect the thrusters, redirect us. I could have done it above, with the keypad, but it's coded, so here I just use the information I got on a data dump about standard Imperial engineering—thank you, vats, glad it wasn't all *Sentience: Don't Worry About It*—

It's hot. Getting hard to see out of my suit's visor with all the condensation. The system should take care of the condensation. It's failing, having lost some regulation circuitry to the projectile weapons. And frying me. My own body is overheating. My rapid breathing strains the oxygen supplies in this suit. My stomach is doing flips from the radiation. My testicles swell to twice their size, aching where the Kurgul queen stabbed them.

There. Rewired. And that should give a basic retrieval sequence to the brain.

Just for good measure, I pull everything that has anything to do with the sense-field as well, which means, if our dreadnought can get a clear shot, they can blow this thing before it gets in range of the Thuzerians—well, other than the ones currently dying here.

Sure enough, the planet-cracker starts to slowly turn, exposing me to the light of the Thuzerian planet, that beautiful green marble, as I return to the Resistance. Turns and—

Aw hell, no, the sequence is trying to self-correct. Some subroutine I didn't anticipate. I yank the wires again—at this point, at least the momentum is pushing it away from the planet, if not back toward the Resistance fleet—and I climb back out along my tether.

And I'm cold. Instantly cold. The sweat that soaked me a moment ago freezes on my skin. Yep, those environmental controls in this suit worked a little too hard. Now they're shutting down. How long until the atmos is all gone? Minutes? Seconds? Freezing to death in my suit, killed by my own sweat.

That's not a good death.

I clamber over the nose of the planet-cracker's shield.

Alsethus is still upright, her boots magnet-locked, bubbles of rapidly freezing blood flowing from holes in her suit. The soldier who killed her bends over the pad, trying to reprogram the planet-cracker.

The Resistance soldier looks up just in time to get my sword through their guts—and then I kick them away. I look down the planet-cracker to see more Resistance troops coming toward me.

I wonder how long I have. My limbs are shaking, they're so cold from the lack of air, the rad poisoning, the exhaustion.

I think of Jaqi's hand on my shoulder.

I think of Alsethus's words. *Life is a gift. Each moment is given us by God, in His mercy.*

"Araskar, this is it," a voice says in my ear, as I lunge and parry with my soulsword. "Our ships are out of range. We can blow the planet-cracker now without damaging the planet."

Ah. I see what they're saying.

I slash through the tether.

I step away from my Resistance opponents—and kick off the edge of the planet-cracker, into the emptiness of space. Kick hard. The kind of velocity that will carry me halfway across the solar system before I die.

For one glorious moment it's all beautiful. I spin backward and catch a glimpse of the Thuzerian planet, the distant blue circle, and then a glimpse of the massive, red, pulsing planet-cracking shard, the shard-fire flying past me, as I fly backward, among more debris, more bodies, more cold, the cold stealing into my suit and sucking out the air, freezing the sweat on my skin and the breath in my lungs—

The Thuzerian dreadnought fires on the planet-cracker. A dozen bright shards spin across space, and connect with their larger brother.

They keep shooting, and the shard gets bigger, a bright red burst in the darkness, until it starts to lose stability.

And then I flip over, and the planet below fills my view for half a second, and again, I go tumbling into the darkness—

Saint Jaqi gives me a broad, beatific smile. She climbs from the painting and reaches out.

So this is death.

7

Jaqi

OKAY, JAQI, THINK LIKE you're a human who thought it was a swell idea to put an ecosphere, and a big fancy city, on a moon made of nothing.

This is a moon made of nothing. Where do we put the guns? And the bandages?

I think real hard about that for at least ten Imperial minutes.

And can't think of a thing. Some spaceways scab I am!

This is a job for a book bug. I en't got the imagination.

I wait until I hear John Starfire walk the other way, continuing down the street in the direction I came from. Hopefully he en't figured out which way I came by the dust I disturbed. There was plenty of dust to disturb, but the funny grav at least means it'll settle in strange patterns.

He was probably right about looking for a more industrial district, but I en't following him.

I keep going through the fine, crystal-looking buildings, taking back ways and forcing myself through the compartments full of the dead, when I can stand it. The dust and the stink are awful. I rifle through cupboards, and under all the beds what don't have skeletons on them.

No weapons. No bandages.

These folk were near Suits themselves. Lots of ports for cybernetic implants, lots of leftover implants that fell out of the dead folk. One house has tanks full of calcified goo on the walls, like some kind of vat for treating a disease or injury. But all these folks are gone. I reckon their Bible didn't say as much against mixing man and machine as the one Kalia carries around, from what I know of Bibles.

I take back to the streets and head toward the node-relay towers. There'll be a launch there. Where there's valuable ship bits, there's weapons to defend them.

And hey, as I get closer, as I move through the grid of streets, under this crazing sense-field dome, I feel something familiar.

There's a node.

Can't explain how I know, but it's the same way I've always known—I can just sense them nodes like I put them there.

Is that what I came through? Would have to be, but it don't feel like a standard node. For one thing, I never met no one could survive a naked trip through pure space, but not only did I survive, so did John Starfire.

I keep on walking, to some huge reverse-cells. Giant, pod-looking things, stretching near up to the lights in the sky. Oldest reverse-cells I ever seen. Antiques! The kind that used five times the space and not even a capacity colony of algae to make oxygen. Bill's reverse-cell was huge, but it would have had over a million cloned microalgal components. These old things used genuine living algae. Whole giant colonies.

Or they did. The algae's all died and leaked out the bottom, a black slime coating the street around the tall metal cells.

So how's this place still got air? They sitting on a catch like Shadow Sun Seven was? Maybe the Jorians rigged up the node to keep on bringing air from the planet below? Maybe that's why it feels funny.

"Miss."

I nearly jump out of the whole evil dome.

It's a Suit!

Leastways, I reckon it has to be. It clings to a spur of crystal tower, like a spider, up above me. And it scuttles down, springs through the low gravity to land on the ground, missing a bit of grace.

They got Suits here?

It shuffles along funny—it's got one mechanical leg I

reckon is its original, long and spindly but built like a human's. The other leg, though, is rough-welded and cobbled together, with a big central joint and segments like a spider's. Wire sprouts out of its belly and twists down its legs. A dozen different appendages sprout from the ring around its head. Looks like it's been trying to fix itself for several centuries.

Reminds me a bit of my father, since it's got a metal face with more wires hanging off like a beard. Given the beard, I decide this one's a "he." His blue mechanical eyes cast a funny look at me. He lets out a long, creaking noise, like his internal fans are all about ready to break.

"Miss, eh—" The thing is wearing a smile, like his face done stuck that way. And other than the recognizable words, everything else he's saying is gunk. "Eh sik tah sah veez."

"Uh, salutes. You a . . ." Wait a moment. This Suit broken? "I been to see the Engineer. I know your people. You can speak to me."

"Miss, eh—" It whirrs and hums, in a way no Suit does.

Despite the sketchy augmentation job he's done on himself, to keep working, I don't see any organic components. Is this an automaton? A real live automaton? All machine?

In the stories, them full automatons were dangerous.

Couldn't be trusted and tried to overthrow their masters.

"You a Suit? What is you?"

"Eh sik tah sah veez."

"I can't understand a burning thing you're saying."

The thing whirrs even louder, like it's processing what I've said, all the circuits on the inside firing and playing together.

"I'm wondering whether or not there's any decent weapons around here? And any decent bandages? Got a fella on my tail who's a lot of trouble." Or, depending on how you act as automaton, I might have to shoot you.

More whirring and processing. And then he says, in a passible imitation of a spaceways accent, "I seek to serve you."

So it's learned how to talk like me. Okay, well, in the stories automatons might be trouble, but so far I got no evidence this thing wants to kill me any more than John Starfire, and as much as little Jaqi heard stories about killer automatons, grown-up Jaqi has stood toe to toe with a lot of killers, and they en't all that impressive anymore. "You got any weapons?"

"Our weapons stores have not been replenished in . . ." He take a moment to process. "Eight hundred years by Earth reckoning."

"Oh. But you have them? You have guns?"

"Records tell me that our stores have all lost containment and exploded."

"Aiya." That right there's the problem with shards in the long term. "Exploded."

"The atmosphere in that area of the lunar colony is compromised. I can aid you with a suit if you are cleared to inspect the damage. Please present clearance."

"So there's space suits I can use to look through them guns?"

He stops again and whirrs for a long time. I feel like I'm watching a wheel spin over and over again as he thinks. "The space suits have been compromised. We have no space suits that are marked as preserved for noncorrosion." His improvised legs rattle.

"Aiya," I say. That right there is also a problem with thousand-year-old space suits.

"Please explain the nature of your inquiry," it says.

"Something stuck?" I en't never dealt with a full automaton. Some bluebloods have them, but most Imperial types don't trust 'em—too close to Suits. "You understand me, ai?"

"Ai. Aiya. Please explain the nature of these words."

"Oh, them's just what you say when you need to give spice to your words."

The automaton whirrs again, and says, "We shall remember. You require medical attention."

I look down, at the blood staining my leg from John

Starfire's last cut. "Let me guess. Your medical bits is compromised by age."

"Our medical supplies are vacuum-sealed, and still able to work on organic matter."

Ah, that's good news. "Lead the way. Don't suppose you have any fresh food?"

Stop and whir. "All food supplies have been compromised by age or vacuum."

It strikes me that this might be another one of old Starfire's traps, but at this point I'm in such pain that I don't care. I can't get him back unless I get all patched.

"What killed all these folk, uh . . ." I reckon I need a name for this fella. "Whirr?"

"All sentient life in Luna City has ceased. Signs indicate a virus. This unit has not been given a designation for the virus."

Like I thought. So it was a virus done it. "How long it been since the virus hit?"

"By Earth reckoning, nine hundred fifty-eight years, eleven months and five days have elapsed."

"Earth reckoning? That like Imperial reckoning?"

"Aiya? We do not understand the reference."

Forget it.

The automaton leads me to a tower that stretches way up into the stars overhead, and presses a few buttons so that a compartment opens on the side. It withdraws a few vacuum-sealed packs, and breaks them open, revealing bandages and a cream that smells mighty funny, despite having been sealed.

I don't care. I take the funny cream and smear it into the gashes John Starfire left in me, and begin wrapping the bandages all around my severed muscles, and groan as the pain comes back new—and with it, more memory-pain, the feeling as though all my life's been turned to shards, bouncing around and exploding in my head.

His memories subside, like a beating that's finally ended. They're trouble to even sort through. I try to let them go through me slowly. It en't easy.

A ship in the Dark Zone.

An agricultural world.

A sword in my hand—

It's hard to sort this business, with my own memory unreliable. At some point he found out about the planet at the center of the Dark Zone, but he found out the truth of what the Shir are as well, and that memory en't coming forward to be useful. His memories feel like trying to keep hold of an angry tomcat.

The cream works a bit like a gel-pack, but a lot slower—I can feel myself starting to knit, but not at the rate synthskin would do it.

"Okay," I say. "How long since there been people here for you to talk to?"

"No living sentient has been here in eight hundred years, Earth reckoning."

"Was that last group human?"

"The last group came from the node connected to Earth."

It is a node bringing air here. "And that's really Earth?" The blue planet has changed its position in the sky, but you can still see it at the edge of the city skyline.

"That is Earth, homeworld of the human race."

"Well, throw me out the airlock." That's where me—at least a part of me—comes from. Earth what was lost, and here I found it. "There still folk down there?"

"We have not intercepted a communication from Earth in two hundred years. The relay remains open."

Hm. Wonder if it's another heap of skeletons down there. Or maybe a paradise, kind of place out of a story? Maybe just a heap of sentients sitting around a fire clubbing each other on the head? That virus would have taken its toll down there too. "Any folk alive down there?"

Whir, whir, buzz. "Sensors indicate a small population of pre-industrial humans."

"They have enough to survive?"

More whirring. And then my new friend projects a mighty shaky holo; showing a fairly cozy little city mapped out. Houses and small lanes, dotted lines that indicate fences for critters; a central pyramid left over from the Jorian days. "Sensors indicate the presence of agriculture and rudimentary arts. Remaining structures are often used for poetry, drama, and religious purposes."

"Huh." Look at that. "Fate's teasing me." Even them people, cavemen survivors of a virus killed everything, get to see shows and relax with fancy folk; it's only me that don't. "So there must be another node in-system, opens up to Joria." My other original home.

"Joria?" The automaton makes a lot of that clicking and whirring, and for a minute I reckon he's stuck and I'd best kick him. But then he says, "This name does not exist in my records."

I laugh. "You're fooling. Or you was tampered with. Jorians? Folk that built the nodes? Your memory can't be that corrupted."

"Jorians." It pauses, and whirrs for so burning long I reckon John Starfire is going to show up, shiv me, and be halfway back home by the time this robot figures out it's missing data. But then it says, "Jorians. Characters in a children's novel published in Imperial Year Zero Minus 268, in the Christian reckoning 2099 Anno Domini, in the Muslim reckoning—"

"Hang on," I say. "Jorians is characters in a novel?"

"It was later a successful interactive comic book franchise."

"Hang on," I say again. "Jorians en't made up! They

built the Empire! And the nodes!"

More whirring. More loading. And finally the automaton says, "I'm afraid I don't understand the question. Aiya."

"You're saying Jorians didn't ever exist."

"They existed as characters in a comic book."

I can't help it—Scurv's words pop into my head. "Them comic books lie."

Whirr actually comes back quickly for this one. Just a second of whirring and then, "Humanity makes a distinction between storytelling and lying. Would you be interested to know some of the distinctions that have been offered by notable poets?"

"What's the difference on them Jorians?"

"They were the subject of stories. Many poets and philosophers argue that stories represent a kind of truth that never happened."

I wish I could buy this fella a drink. "That sounds about like the truth I hear." I take a deep breath of Earth's own air, and say, "So the Jorians was . . ."

"A story."

-8-

Kalia

MY FATHER HAD MANY sayings, but I always thought this one was especially apt: you cannot live anyone else's life. Even for crosses, who take others' memories with their swords, he used to say, someone else's life isn't lived, just seen through a filter of violence.

That's why Jaqi underestimated me, and still hasn't guessed that I stowed away on her ship to the Dark Zone. That's why I am now stuck in a very cramped closet, trying not to move around too much.

Jaqi took one look at me and decided that I was some kind of fancy girl who only cared about fashions. I know that's the spaceways stereotype of people like me: bluebloods who spend all their considerable money on their clothes and their hair. Gullible and stupid and easily killed if only we could be separated from our money.

It's not true.

Well, it was. It's not anymore. I've learned a few things from the Red Peace.

The door opens. I smell the cigar.

"We are ready, girl."

"You shouldn't smoke those in here," I say. "They tax the air filters."

Scurv Silvershot laughs at me. I get the feeling that vi has been laughing at me a lot, but I don't really care. I stretch out my legs. Ow.

"Where's Jaqi?" I say. "Did you, uh—did you tell her?"

"The Girl of Stars is inside the temple," Scurv says.

"Inside the temple? But you said there's no way to get in there. You were sure we would need the Pet."

"We were wrong." Vi shrugs, a weird catlike movement that looks more like vi's shaking off water from fur.

"You spent a year trying to get in there! And Jaqi just walks in?"

"We suppose what John Starfire says is true. There's some crosses more pure than others. It scanned Jaqi's hand and let her in." Again, that twisting shrug. "We thought we would let her try the entrance, then we could explain why we brought you. But now it will not let either of us in, without your pet."

"The Pet," I correct vim automatically, and then cringe. I'm trying not to do that. Jaqi hates it when I correct her.

"Come on now." Vi seems unbothered by corrections.

We go down the gangplank into a night without stars. The sky is completely dark, a solid wall of black above us. I guess I knew it would be that way, but it makes me shiver. Even on cloudy nights at home, you didn't get the sense of such a dark sky.

The ocean crashes against the rocks, and the floodlights from our ship light up a long causeway across the water, the churning tide around us, and the outline of what must be the gate to the temple, illuminated by the flickering sense-field.

"What keeps the—*them* away from the planet?"

"Don't rightly know that. If we did, we would export it," vi says. "Best we can say it, there's something on this planet causes them pain."

"Pain? To the . . . to *them*." Dad always said there wasn't going to be any consequences for just saying *Shir*, but I can't bring myself to say it. They're as close as the nearest star system. The nightmares that used to keep me from sleep for weeks at a time. "*They* can move faster than light, but it's not the same system of nodes we have." Everyone knows that. "The Navy tried to kill *them* at their expansion points, where *their* network might expand."

"That's right, girl. Devils could be here in seconds, if they wished, but they do not ahh—" Vi lets out a grunt, hunches over in front of me.

"What is it?"

"Uh, speaking of pain, we've got a bit of a headache ourselves." Scurv grimaces, speaking through clenched teeth.

"Uh, I'm sorry . . ."

"En't a thing. It passes." In the darkness, I can only see faint movements, but it looks like Scurv is holding vir head.

I keep the Pet in its box. I know it's a Suit, if not one of the sentient ones, because it perks up whenever there's machinery around. It skitters inside its case, bouncing off the walls of the box. It reminds me of when Quinn tried to hide a puppy in his room, when we were a lot younger and Toq was a baby. The puppy went nuts every time she smelled food.

And Father was still alive, though I won't think on that. And I knew where Mother was, and didn't wonder if she might be freezing to death in some black mining operation in the wild worlds.

I can't afford to think about that.

I haven't even told Jaqi that I think my mother might be alive. At first I thought she might be with the people we rescued from Shadow Sun Seven, but it was only my uncle Staran, who lived most of the time on Irithessa; no one from Keil must have been taken in that group. My mother and father were separated, on different sides of the planet when the Resistance attacked. I have no idea what happened to her.

"So there's the sense-field. Came down long enough to let Jaqi in, then popped up fast enough to keep us from getting in." Scurv chews the cigar, seeming unbothered that it's gone out. "You want to try your pet?"

I walk along the causeway, the wind whipping ocean spray onto me as I go. I'm wet and cold by the time I get to the sense-field, but it doesn't matter. We don't know what's in there, and Jaqi went in alone.

"Right there," vi says, pointing to the flickering light of a scan-box.

"She just stuck her hand in there. And it opened."

"She the Chosen One, en't she, aiya?"

I let the Pet out of its box and put it into the scan-box for the gate, and it skitters around, like a spider, throwing out a dozen different spindly black appendages into the ancient machinery. After a very long time, and several strange buzzes and whines, the sense-field vanishes.

And the Pet lets out a long, keening whine, and curls up.

"Are you okay?" I say, and cradle it.

Scurv steps through where the sense-field was. "What happened to your pet, girl?"

"I don't know. This old tech hurts it." The Pet smells burned, and it is curling up against me like an injured puppy.

I follow vim into the courtyard of the temple, where it's impossible to see anything save the vague outline of the temple overhead, illuminated by our ship's floodlights.

"Is it badly damaged?" vi asks.

"Can't really say."

"We have dealt with Suits before. Let us give it a look," Scurv says, lighting an emergency bulb that briefly blinds me. While I'm blinking away the light, vi takes the Pet—and extinguishes the bulb.

It's not totally dark, though. I can see vir angular face, though—illuminated by the green gleam coming from vir gun. "Scurv, what are you doing? Are you charging up a shard to *see* by?"

Scurv sighs. "Please understand, girl," vi says. "We do not like this part of the job."

"What?" That's when I realize the gun is pointed at me.

"Scurv, no—"

"Don't argue, girl. Make peace with your god, aiya?" Vi gestures with the gun. "Go on. We'll count to three."

"No, I can't—" I need to run, but where can I run from someone who never misses a shot? "Why are you doing this? For the Pet? What about Jaqi? Are you going to—"

"We don't like when it's children. Tell that to your god for us, aiya?" The green shard in vir gun is blazing now, lighting up the pale, angled contours of vir face. "In our next life, no children and guns. One. Two."

No, I can't—I came all this way because Jaqi is the Son of Stars, I—

"Ah!" Scurv's face twists in pain.

I run.

And Scurv misses me. God be praised. Vi misses me, the best shot in the galaxy, so that headache must be something—

I run through the gate, along the causeway, and realize my only chance is the water. The water, crashing against the rocks, which will probably slice me apart—but that's better than a shard! I jump in.

Instant cold, and the water is bitter and acidic and why—ow—that's a rock I just hit my head on, I think I might be bleeding, I need some air—I need to—no, I need to swim, even if I'm bleeding. I swim. I swim into the tide. When the waves lift me up I try to dive down, under them. Just dive under the waves, just like bodysurfing on a nice day on Keil, even bleeding, even—

Green flashes erupt around me. Scurv's shards. I keep swimming. My chest hurts so much it feels like something is going to tear out of it, and another wave slams me into a rock that rips my side open—

And suddenly I'm being sucked down.

Oh no—no—I'm going to drown, going to die here—

The water crushes me against smooth tunnel walls, pushes the air out of my lungs as I go down, and tumble, and smack my head again and I almost open my mouth but some part of my brain yells *No, don't do that*—

I open my eyes against the stinging salt and see a light. I push myself through the water toward the light even though it hurts. Everything hurts. It all hurts so much, and I'll never find Mom, I'll never see Toq, and Quinn will have died for nothing—*no, keep swimming, keep swimming, God hears you, swim!*

I surface at the bottom of a narrow, dark well.

I gag and puke seawater. There's a few faint lights far above that have the look of emergency bulbs someone's strung around.

"Ow." I lift my hand up, and though I can't see it, I can tell my arm is bleeding. Probably every part of me is bleeding.

I'm under the temple, I think. The open area above me is inside. I was swept in here through the tunnels that let in seawater.

Ladders rise up the side, out of the water. I grab one and my hand immediately slips—it's slick with native algae. I try again, keeping my grip despite the slippery algae.

The pain is pretty bad, as soon as I get out of the water and take a breath. I'm bleeding a lot.

Dad would say that counting your blessings will always make things better, even if it's a short count. So, I'm bleeding and hurt, but the saltwater cleaned the wounds. Scurv wants to kill me, and vi is one person you can trust to kill, but at least vi has a headache. I have a ladder out of here. There might be medical supplies . . . somewhere.

Weirdly, I do feel better. Thanks, Dad.

Up I go.

The ladder rungs get more reliable as I go, less algae-eaten. There's strong plastisteel underneath the algae, it just hasn't been cleaned in a long time. After a while climbing, I realize I'm pretty far above the water, and falling from this height might be as bad as falling onto a hard surface. Plus, my hands are shaking and I'm pretty sure I'm more soaked with blood than with salt water . . . but I keep going.

I have to keep going.

I'll find Jaqi, and tell her Scurv betrayed us, and then we'll get out of here, and we'll find where Mom is.

It gives me strength. I keep climbing.

I finally reach another beveled edge, and clamber up another set of ladders, much shorter, and find myself in the main hallway of what I think is this temple.

It's been a while since anyone was in here. Other than a few distinct scuffs, there's dust thick on everything.

Footprints show sign of a struggle. A bridge spans the pit I climbed up from, and the dust there is freshly disturbed. Somebody dragged something. There's stains on the floor too. Looks like blood. Not mine.

I follow the path into what used to be some kind of

control room for this place. And—by some miracle—

"Oh God. Oh my God, thank you, thank you God." I'm not sure if I'm praying or babbling. Someone's left an open first-aid kit here, with gel-packs for restoring flesh—the kind of thing you use on crosses. Right in the middle of the room!

They're meant for crosses, but they'll work for humans.

I tear open the gel-packs and rub them into every scrape I can find on my body. It's not easy to cover all the scrapes. I have gashes all along my arms and my butt and my back and my neck is raw and red and I'm lucky I have no open arteries from all those sharp rocks.

There's something weird about the seawater here. Most of the wetness on me is blood, which means the planet's atmosphere is drier than it seems, maybe too nitrogen-rich. It's the kind of thing that terraforming engineers would have to keep coming back to and correcting. But for me, it means that I didn't leave a big wet trail on the ground, just some blood. Hopefully it dries quickly too, blending in with the blood already there.

"Thank you, God," I whisper.

Scurv won't know I was in here, if I'm careful and hide my footprints.

One of my shoes has also been slashed to ribbons, so I take the shoe off, and pack gel around the top of the foot, the synthskin slowly grafting onto the real skin. I don't like the idea of going barefoot—vi'll be able to pick out my small feet. I tear my shirt and wrap my bare foot in the raggedy pieces and look around for some place to hide. The gel-packs are quite warm. They'll make me sleepy.

There's several heavy boxes and cases piled in a corner, all of them against each other. I manage to get around one, and slink into a spot small enough that maybe Scurv won't be able to fit there either.

Father's voice comes to me, and Quinn's too. Telling me why I couldn't be involved with their meetings. *Kalia, you'll understand the Resistance, soon enough. As soon as you turn fourteen.*

Ha. My birthday is still a few Imperial months off. Fourteen, my cut-up shoeless foot.

And then the gel-packs take effect and I fall dead asleep.

It's really good that I've been running around robbing prisons and fighting the Vanguard, because I just barely wake up when Scurv comes in.

"Damn thing," Scurv says to the Pet. "Patch me in."

I recognize the skittering noise.

Vi might have been here for a while. Why hasn't vi seen me? Surely Scurv would scope out a room before vi did anything there. In all the holos and comic books about vim, nobody's dead until the body's cold in the center of the screen.

"Ah—ow. Ah."

Scurv's headache still going, I see. Is vi really getting this careless over a headache? I mean, I'm impressed with how far I've managed to come today, but vi should have hit me the first time vi tried it. I'm just a kid.

And then—the unmistakable whir and hum of a node-relay opening.

"I'm in a firefight here," a voice says, weirdly calm for what it's saying.

"We can't find any trace of either of them," Scurv says, and vir voice sounds shaky. That must be a serious hangover. Or something worse. Vi didn't seem like vi was in pain before. Is it something about this planet? Something about the Shir?

"Did they kill each other?"

Scurv actually laughs. "So cold, to be talking about your love."

"Yes, well, my love ordered someone in the fleet to take preemptive action, against my orders, and I'm facing the wrath of the entire Thuzerian Order. Don't leave until you have two corpses." That's cold. "Two Sons of Stars, both dead."

"Dead now? You said incapacitated. After he got what he wanted from her, aiya."

"I changed my mind. Find them both. Bring me the corpses."

"Your own husband."

"I was told that you asked no questions, just took the money."

Who is Scurv talking to? Who wants to kill her husband? There's only one other Son of Stars I've heard of besides Jaqi, and that's John Starfire. Is he talking to John Starfire's wife, Aranella? She is supposed to be the Resistance's right hand.

Scurv says in that pained voice, "No trouble. We've killed lots of Chosen Ones."

I try not to make any noise as Scurv shuts off the relay.

Scurv was just ordered to kill Jaqi *and* John Starfire. By John Starfire's wife.

Well. I either have to stop Scurv from that, or better yet, get vim to tell me everything. Which means I need to disarm vim and find some way to hold it over vir head. A thirteen-year-old girl, outsmarting the famous sheriff of all the wild worlds.

This is a lot of delicate work, Dad would say, when he was trying to explain why I couldn't know about what he did with his crosses. Don't I, cut up and cowering behind a stack of boxes on the side of the most dangerous person in the galaxy, know it.

9

Jaqi

CONVERSATION TAKES A WHILE with Whirr. I ask a question, his servos and gears spin and he sits there retrieving the answer. Reminds me of the Engineer, but at least he's got the sense not to look like a centipede, even with them extra loader-arms and bits sticking on him.

"Look, I'm trying to figure out a way to kill the . . ." I have to say it. I reckon I called their attention down on me plenty of times already. "What's in your system about the . . ." Oh hell, Jaqi, it en't like they haven't already noticed you. "Shir."

"Sheer? We can access numerous sheer leggings that will compress and flatter—"

"Shir! The devils!" I shudder saying it, and even though I en't religious, my hands automatically cross my heart to protect against evil.

More whirring. A long, loud whir and then Whirr says, "Shir is a common shorthand in corrupted Martian creole for pure-space beings."

"Aiya, that's it. Evil corruption on them. Look like big old spiders the size of suns. They swallow suns and gas giants, use them to power their guts. They move faster than light, but it en't the same network of nodes we use." Hang on a second. "You said pure-space beings?"

A long, long whirring sound as his gears turn, and he says, "We have detailed information on pure-space beings, but it is encoded."

"You mean I can't see it?"

"I must take you to the Archives tower and access central memory through a hard connection. Wireless emitters have degraded."

"Archives tower." Shit, I don't want that, I want the weapons stores, but since they've apparently blown up, I guess we'll do this in the library.

I am destined to spend all my days with book bugs.

He's got a working—just barely—car. En't nothing fancy, just wheels and seats, but he drives me through the city under the lattice-light dome, old Earth that was lost following us across the horizon as we go, its light playing off the crystal towers that rise around us. I don't ask no more questions as we go, as the stuff that's in my wounds makes me sleepy.

I near drift off, but every time I do, I remember John Starfire is somewhere in this city, and he's probably got his own helper automaton by now.

That'll keep a girl awake.

I see what I reckon is the Archives Tower on the horizon. Far off the horizon, outside the domed city. As we go, the dry, airless gray soil of this moon outside the sense-field grows closer. Right outside the sense-field, and nothing there but a bare rock in bare vacuum.

It still don't make a lick of sense. Who builds on a place like this?

Humans should have known better than to try it, especially once they sussed out terraforming, aiya? But maybe by the time the Jorians taught them terraforming they done had all this built anyway.

Or maybe Whirr's right and there weren't no Jorians. Maybe everything—crosses, Suits, even humanoid sentients—maybe that's all one race making trouble for itself.

Could it be? I en't no book bug, but I know that even species that seem real weird, like Zarra, started as crosses. Fluid sentients and crickets crossed with humankind, too, back when races first started to mix it up.

Or maybe that Jorians is a story people started because it helped give the Empire, the bluebloods, some credibility. Maybe it was easier to pass off the cross armies dying in the Dark Zone if you said they was part warriors from the ages past.

But burning hell and the devil, what a thing to be wrong about.

We reach what seems to be the end of the sense-field, and then we pass underground, driving through a tunnel full of flickering lights, past more automatons carefully repairing things. Funny-looking automatons this time—just little rolling boxes with spindly arms—but nothing as funny as what I seen on the Suits' planet.

We emerged into a wide chamber with a forest of pillars, all of them blinking softly. Pillars march on forever into a cold, white chamber. They vanish overhead, into the darkness of the ceiling. Faint lights glimmer above me too. Thin, spindly walkways cross between the pillars, all the way up, made of that same crystal material that makes up the rest of the city.

"Huh," I say. "Whole place is a memory-crypt?"

"This is the Archives Tower," Whirr says. "I can permit you access to all public records stored here. Authorization codes will be required for private information."

"This whole place is full of information." And was just waiting? "This can't be. Folk've been looking for this information for a thousand years. They always said the devils ate whole planets full of libraries and things and I was told there weren't many records left of Earth, and the Jorians . . ." The Suits would get positively slacky here. So would every book bug in the spaceways. All that information lost to the First Empire, right here!

"Read at your leisure."

"Read. Ah, right," I say. Reading again. I promise, Kalia, I'll listen next time. "Why don't you just read it to me?"

"What would you like me to read?"

"Anything that tells about them first nodes." Whirr blinks, and does his namesake again. "You know, the ones the—the first time folk traveled faster than light."

"Are you speaking of the Contact?" Whirr takes a minute to do his namesake, and then says, "The Contact is the name commonly given to what occurred between genetically modified humans and a race of quantum-dimensional beings, preparing a path for faster-than-light travel and the construction of the first Intergalactic Congress."

"Yep, that sounds right," I say. Genetically modified humans? There was crosses ten thousand years ago in the First Empire too? And still no Jorians, 'cept the ones he says is made up. "Start there, and go till you get to them . . . devils and how to get rid of them."

He only takes about a minute to start reading me a batch of jargon. "During the first days of the Earth-Mars alliance, the rigors of Mars colonization led to a greater interest in genetic modification. Heavy exploration of brain modification led to some theorization that, as was done with quantum computers, even human memories could take advantage of quantum storage. Those who attempted this modification soon reported that they were communicating with an extra-dimensional race who existed in a state of quantum flux. This seemed specious at first, but many years of experimentation proved that a node could be opened to this dimension, and by passing through points in this dimension, humans could travel via wormhole faster than light."

"There weren't no Jorians in that, Whirr," I say.

"Jorians. A fictional species from a successful comic book franchise—"

"What happened next?"

Whirr does it again—gets stuck. And finally, after a real long bout of his namesake, he says what I heard before—"The Empire spread across thirteen galaxies, and further, with hundreds of thousands of nodes, well over a million planets terraformed. And then..." He keeps whirring. "And then..."

"And then the Empire died." I remember that bit.

"We do not have treatment for the virus." Whirr appears stuck. "We do not have treatment for the virus. We have done our best, but any human DNA is vulnerable. We do not have treatment..."

And there he gets stuck.

So let me get this straight. Humans—not Jorians, just

humans—made contact with creatures in pure space.

The First Empire was a good thirteen galaxies wide.

And a virus came along?

Whirr does his namesake for a good ten Imperial minutes, which is to say the longest minutes of all. And then, of a sudden, he pops out, "I have found a holo, beamed back via node from another galaxy."

He projects a figure again, and it looks like just a human, and this human takes a breath and speaks—and I know he's speaking of my galaxy.

"I am beaming this message back to the planet designated TS-101. The virus has taken hold of our crew. The other ships in the fleet have not survived after they tried to reason with the . . . with *them*."

I've seen this holo afore.

No, wait—John Starfire seen it.

The memory matches up. John Starfire, having survived battle in the Dark Zone, having found a ship, much older than any other ship in that combat zone, and a holo that told an old secret.

He connects more wires, checks more control panels, and at last the archived message appears before him. And tells him a secret the entire Empire has forgotten.

The John Starfire in memory, and the Jaqi of now, both of us listen.

"*They* can't be reasoned with. *They* don't remember what

they were." He's talking about the devil. Only one thing in the universe folk talk about that way. "*Their* transition into this dimension has taught *them* only hunger. The lost suns are proof of this." The man's face is haggard, and marked with blotches. Disease has rooted in the man's body, it is clear. "Once *they* opened all of space to us. Once *they* were the music of the stars. It appears we can still use the nodes, but there will be no new nodes. The sensitives among us go mad ... when *they* come near."

I'm confused and curious, and in memory, John Starfire is too.

Is he saying that the devil—the Shir used to be the *Starfire* itself? They was really pure-space beings?

How'd they change?

The memory answers me. "It seems that, when the human sensitives bonded to—to *them* died, *they* breached the dimensional wall, to try and reach *their* symbiotes in our universe. *They* weren't made for it.

"This is a message to the crew on TS-101. Keep the experiment going. The unique fold in pure space around that planet means that you may yet be able to bring one to maturity without losing it. The children are the key. The children are the key."

The holo crackles and becomes inaudible.

I stand there staring like an idiot.

And John Starfire's memory matches me. *He can only*

sit and stare. This is the origin of the Dark Zone, revealed.

TS-101 is a First Imperial designation for a planet. It sounds like the place they were trying to breed more of the pure-space beings. He could find it, if he could find a star-map of the Dark Zone before the Shir came.

The truth is overwhelming. For this all his friends and family died? For this great secret: the Shir were not always what they are.

The Empire must fall. For this secret, it must.

He stands before a mirror and cuts his face, wedges synth-skin into it, cuts it again. To make a new face, to overthrow an Empire with.

I huddle down as well, just as bowled over as John Starfire in the memory. "Oh hell." The entire galaxy, open to folk, and then the Starfire people, the people made up of pure space, they got turned into the devils.

"One moment, please," Whirr says, and cocks his little automatic head to the side. "One moment."

"What you talking about?"

"Another patron to the Archives has requested your presence, Miss Jaqi."

My blood goes cold. Another patron? He found me? Already?

"Little spaceways girl. Went as far as you could, I'll give you that." John Starfire walks toward me through the pillars.

10

Z

THE TRACE SYSTEM IS still bucolic from a distance, the planet gleaming, its moon a speck in the sky, welcoming the traveler. Last time I was here, I died slowly, my body rotting away inside from the NecroWasp's poison. I thought only of meeting my ancestors with honor.

Now I am unkillable, and thus cut off from honor.

I did not appreciate how good it could be, dying of poison.

"Well, look who it is!"

Swez, of the Matakas, appears on my viewscreen, unchanged. "I had money down that at least one of you would survive Shadow Sun Seven. And here you are. Without tattoos! You survived, but got those tattoos removed? Wouldn't've put money on that part, myself."

"Swez." It takes a minute to even address someone so dishonorable. And I do not like to be reminded, to see my skin without the names of my fathers and grandfathers. A reminder of the things done to my honor. My skin is pale white, unmarred, like a babe's, and truly a confusing thing to look upon. I feel as though I have been in another womb, and need to earn my honor afresh. "You have committed one of the most dishonorable acts I have ever heard tell of," I say to him.

"I know." He rattles his annoying wings again. "At least by your perception. Would love to have you discuss it with my ethics class. I'll have you in as a guest speaker."

"You." This takes a moment to absorb, even for one as familiar with dishonor as me. "You are teaching *ethics*? To Kurguls?"

"Comparative ethics. To everyone! Lots of money to be made with the new, John-Starfire-approved curriculum. We're going to try and seed the curriculum, then copy-protect it so anyone who uses it will have to pay."

Even in a newly reformed galaxy, that cannot be legal. Then again, legality rarely reflects honor. "I must land on Trace," I say. "And speak with the Engineer."

"Yeah? Give me a reason why I shouldn't shoot you down."

"You wish to gain Jaqi's favor, and the favor of the Reckoning back, do you not?" I wait to see if this registers. The truth is, I am not good at bluffing. It seems like good bargaining material, but it is only stating the obvious.

I never figure such things out until after I have said them.

"She survived too?"

"She is . . ." There is little dishonor in lying to someone who will not do honorable things with your own words. "She is a confirmed Saint. Her miracles abound. If she wished to, she could throw your planet in the sun."

"You're a terrible liar!" He laughs so hard that the rattle of his vestigial wings drowns out his laughter. "You're such a bad liar that I think I'll let you land. The Engineer's been asking after you folk."

"So we did not need to have this conversation." I am glad that my newfound abilities are only restricted to my own body, and I have not the powers Jaqi does, to manipulate nodes.

If I could, I would create a node between my fist and Swez's face.

And I would use it to punch him.

(In case that was not clear.)

After an easy flight, I step from the shuttle onto the Suits' world. My second time here.

As before, the air is noxious with the fumes of several billion machines. They crawl around me, bulbous shapes with insectile legs, flesh half revealed in miles of circuitry. Their vat-towers reach to the sky, bearing sentient bodies for harvest. The Suits' mainframe is as hideous as it was before, as much a product of dishonorable practices, pushing away truth, ancestors, natural resource, and replacing the world with machines.

I step into the central chamber. Such an easy return, to a place we earned with such pain. When we came before, I was poisoned, we were hungry and running from the Vanguard and the Dark Zone. Now I should come as one who has conquered death, who has been through many great battles, not as one betrayed. Yet here I am. Betrayed, dishonored, yet unafraid.

I can already tell it is not here.

My honor is not one of the smears on the walls, or one of the machine-men emerging from that wall, or the smears of yellow in the atmosphere that denote the nano-Suit swarms. It could not be here. The Suits have in-sulated themselves against honor.

My honor is still on Shadow Sun Seven, and still in Araskar's hands.

And on Zarra-kr-Zar, with my people.

"You have returned."

The Engineer seems older, as much as I cannot say why, and thus would not speak such a thought aloud. "You return." His many segments rattle and click along his body, and he twists in place. His voice is as flat and devoid of passion as ever, showing how far he has gone from any notion of true sentience, which is linked to true honor. "You return to give us your data?"

"Don't mock my honor." I point a finger—a finger that

mocks all of us, as it is white and unmarred, where it previously bore a part of my great-great-great-grandfather's name. "You have changed me!"

"I . . ." The Engineer takes a moment to reply, and I await his answer. It would be a shame to kill something so ancient, but I will if I must. "I have done nothing save what we bargained."

"What had your bargain to do with me?"

"Nothing," he says. "I bargained with the girl. Her alone. You we have not touched. And yet . . ." More words, more memories, flash before his eyes. "Yet you contain within you multitudes of ours."

"I did not seek this!"

"Neither did we."

That is a peculiar answer.

"A shipment of our smallest selves, bearers of microscopic data, vanished from our very air, shortly after we saw you." He pauses. "They are inside you now. They are part of you. I cannot say how."

"You know how! You wanted my memories, my most sacred things, but—" Wait. I stop myself.

Jaqi's first miracle I could not explain, except to attribute it to the ancestors, until I learned the truth of how the Suits did it. But her second was of a kind with her skills—moving a node. Is it possible? Did Jaqi, not knowing what she did, open a node inside me and bring nano-Suits to heal me?

Did *Jaqi* do this to me?

If so, I have an even more complicated situation here. If your mate unknowingly compromises your honor, the issue must go before the elders. It can take years to determine a course of action. Never mind the fact that Jaqi will never again consider herself my mate.

I do not even know how to begin explaining this to my elders.

Of course it is Jaqi who complicates my honor!

"Tell me what you hypothesize," the Engineer says. "We allowed you to land because of the data. We will not speak any longer unless you share data."

I tell him my newly conceived theory. "I believe that the nano-Suits came through a node. A node inside . . ." I touch the center of my chest, where there was once a puckered scar from the stinger that killed me. "Inside of me."

The Engineer waits, perhaps absorbing this data. "A micro-node. Fragments of the oldest data speak of them. As instruments of healing, of building, and as weapons."

"That would be a fearsome weapon, and one that could not be used without some dishonor."

"Our smallest gatherers of data are now fused with you. They are a part of your data."

I grit my teeth. Had I my way, I would kill the Engineer

for his part in this, but that would not be honorable either. "I want you to remove them. This is not who I am!"

"It cannot be done." The Engineer rears up a bit, metal legs creaking. I think I see flesh, ancient, pockmarked flesh, inside that metal body. "They have merged with you. It is the way of the galaxy. Flesh and steel merge. One being merges with another. One being crosses with another. It has been done a thousand times, a thousand different ways. All data tells us this. All memory."

"Does data tell you that it is wrong? That it is dishonorable? My people are made by our land, by our traditions, by our ancestors!"

"Your people." The Engineer again flashes numbers and letters across his screen. "Your people, data tells me, suffer greatly. A virus reported on Zarra-kr-Zar."

I am forced to turn my face, not to show my sorrow to my enemy.

I am too late. Zarra-kr-Zar was to be my next stop, to warn my people about the Faceless Butcher's plan to unleash the digger virus again. He will have already sent agents there, to make up for what was done on Shadow Sun Seven.

"In exchange for your data, we will give you more of our smallest parts. The ones you call nano-Suits." The Engineer makes this sound so pale, so casual. As if it were not a violation of all honor. "They can heal your people.

They can become one. Flesh and steel."

"This is dishonorable. We would rather die honorably."

"Data suggests that codes of honor are often reinterpreted based on new developments. Data also suggests that few cultures who prize honor consider death by disease to be a preferred mode of death."

"Data is not honor." If it were, data would have fallen on its sword.

"You had data relating to the Dark Zone. We have a piece of data we have not shared. We can offer it in good faith."

"What is this?" I ask. "What do you mean? You know something about Abaddon you have not told us?" This, perhaps, I could use to redeem my honor. Jaqi is destined to defeat the children of giants, the Great Spiders, but the method of her destiny was not known to her.

"The Shir use a web of dark nodes, their own unique faster-than-light network, which cannot be understood, or navigated," the Engineer says. "Unlike our system of nodes, they create new points of faster-than-light travel when they consume a sun. But in person, they use radio waves to communicate."

A strange, mottled sound, like a choked scream, comes from the Engineer. It raises hackles on every inch of my skin. It is surely one of the most hideous sounds ever heard. "What is that?"

"That is Shir song," the Engineer says.

"They sing," I say.

"They communicate via node-relay and radio wave, but it cannot be interpreted with any data available. This we can interpret: some is speech, some, we think, is song."

The Great Spider sings. Abaddon itself, Hell itself, sings. I wonder whether that will matter to Jaqi. "What do you ask in return for a file of their song?"

The Engineer does not answer. He waits so long, in fact, that I worry he is about to have me killed, or otherwise removed from the planet.

"New data," he finally says, in a garbled voice.

"What is this?" I say. "Are you done speaking to me?"

"New data." I almost think I hear emotion in that voice. A hint of fear? It cannot be, for the Engineer has quenched his feeling.

"There is a black spot on our sun."

Kalia

Scurv doesn't hear me. Vi doesn't even look for me. Vi staggers, lurching from side to side, clutching vir head as vi goes out the door.

My breathing sounds as loud as thunder. Gel-packs can make you ignore your injuries while they're still knitting, so I try to move carefully, and quietly, and sneak out of the corner. But even if I were lying on the ground moaning, I'm not sure Scurv would notice me. Vi staggers across the bridge and back out the entrance of the temple—all the time not seeing me as I sneak after vim.

The sun has come up outside, just enough to illuminate the causeway in dawn gray. The waves still crash against the causeway, with less force. It all looks really pretty, actually.

Scurv makes vir way across the causeway and I feel awful and exposed, but I keep sneaking after vim and vi just never looks back to see me, just staggers forward, clutching vir head.

Vi nearly collapses, leaving the causeway to walk along the beach. Clutching at a tree branch, vi forces vimself up, gasps for air. Vi staggers along the beach, to a hut. Unlike the weatherbeaten structure of the temple, this one looks kind of recent. It must have been vir shelter when vi was stuck on the planet before. It looks like the sticks and mud have been layered over a prefabbed hut, the kind of thing that can be folded up into a box.

I creep closer.

I can almost hear Toq saying *We should go back*. And I think of Father, and Mother, both of them saying, *You don't change the Empire by being safe.*

I creep along the beach to the door of the hut, drop to my knees, and peer inside the crack in the door.

A low, flickering light illuminates a weird lab. In the center there is a long tube, clear. The contents of the tube look like the inside of the disposal on Shadow Sun Seven, all folds of flesh and things that look like organs, pulsating.

Gross, gross, that disposal tube is still the grossest thing in space.

Scurv, hands shaking, whispers, "There, my lovelies. There we are. Change now, we can."

And vi actually sets vir guns down on a table that abuts the tube of weird fleshy bits—and opens the guns. Huh. Never thought I'd see that.

With shaking hands, swathed in thick gloves, vi lifts out the Skithr symbionts from inside vir guns.

They look like bits cut from the mines in Shadow Sun Seven as well. Just little flaps of flesh, but they're glowing faintly green. That'll be the synthetic unthunium they excrete.

Scurv, hands shaking worse than ever, keys a sequence into the weird, pulsating tube, and reaches in and pulls out two little lumps of flesh.

Oh my gosh.

I know what vi's doing—vi's gotten vir symbionts to

reproduce. Those little bits of fresh flesh in vir hands, taken from the vat in the center of the hut, are the children. The ones vi took out of the gun are the previous generation.

Of course! This has to be the most secure planet in the galaxy. Skithr symbionts are impossibly valuable.

And I know I have to get them. This will be my only chance to disarm Scurv.

Maybe it's from hanging out with Jaqi and Z, but I don't hesitate. I leap into the room, and Scurv sees me, and looks at vir guns, which are currently useless, and frantically tries to stick the babies back in that incubation chamber with shaking hands and—

I kick vim in the back of the knees. It's not very nice, but neither is trying to shoot me.

"The lovelies!" The baby Skithrs drop to the ground. I reach, and the sleep has done me good, because my hands don't shake when I grab them.

I come up to find that I'm facing Scurv, who is holding a regular old everyday shard-blaster in one hand, shaking so badly that the red glow makes a blur in the air.

"You're not going to shoot me," I say, holding up the small, pulsating baby symbionts. They're already glowing green, and I hope they don't produce their synthetic shards when scared. It would be dumb to blow my hands off.

"Put our lovelies down, girl!" Scurv's voice is hoarse and weak. "We will shoot you."

"Well, the comic books would say you never miss," I say, looking at vir shaking hands, and holding the baby Skithr symbionts to my chest, and trying not to show how I'm shaking too. "So you should be able to shoot my head off without harming your lovelies."

Scurv makes a weak little sound and collapses back, against the incubation chamber vi got the babies from.

"But them comic books lie."

Scurv gasps out, like they're vir last words, "Them comic books lie."

"Who were you talking to back there?"

"We was hired to do a job." Vi gasps in pain. "No more Chosen Ones."

"Who hired you?"

"Starfire's wife. Wants them both dead, aiya." Scurv blinks. "They'll attach to you, girl. They must, or die in the next few minutes."

I look down and vi's right—the symbionts are trying to crawl up my arms now, and putting out little suckers to attach to me.

"Take care of my lovelies, girl. Knew this was a risk too big to take…"

I drop the baby symbionts onto the table next to their dying forebears, and Scurv winces, tries to get up. "I want more information than what I could get just listening to you. I want to know what you're not telling us. About this planet. About the Shir. Anything!"

"We don't know that." Scurv's voice is now just a whisper. "Found this place by luck. Was a good place to grow new lovelies. Lost the coordinates when we jumped out of Dark Zone, when we ran straight into Imperial patrol, thrown in jail. Didn't lie about that."

"Where does John Starfire come into this?"

"Starfire's wife hired us after we left Shadow Sun Seven. We made contact with her." Vi tries to get up and fails. "Please, girl!"

I've never had to make a decision like this before.

Vi defended us. Vi saved us from the Vanguard. "Why did you betray us?"

Scurv blinks. "Good money in betrayal," vi says, before vir eyes start to fade.

"I thought you had a code of honor. You always do, in the . . ." Never mind.

"It is who I am."

That settles it.

I put the symbionts inside the guns, and small suckers emerge from the bottom of the gun hilts. Without really thinking, I press the hilts of the guns against my waist, and feel a weird sucking sensation as the symbionts bond to me. "No need to go unarmed anymore."

The withered tubes that lead to Scurv's body kink and tear, first one and the other as I hold the guns in my shaking hands.

I raise the gun and Scurv nods. "We thank you for doing it quick."

"Thank you, for teaching me something important."

I shoot Scurv dead.

This is the first person I've killed in this war. A helpless, quivering person I thought was a friend.

I don't feel any regret. I feel like I've finally fought back.

11

Araskar

MY EYELIDS CRAWL OPEN, and I see only a blur. A white haze, spread between goo filling the crevices of my eyelids.

I start to breathe by reflex, and can't do it. Something is holding me back from breathing. Oh. Maybe it's this big machine in my mouth, the tubes running down my throat. It vibrates, sucking goo out of my lungs. And I realize, weirdly, that I don't need to breathe yet. My body has all the nutrients that breathing would provide already.

The machine pulls away, and I become aware of my ears, which hear the hum of the automation through more layers of goo. Little automated limbs clean the goo from my skin.

My last thoughts drift across my mind, like the memory of a dream. *So this is death.*

So this is . . . birth?

I'm in a vat? I've been reborn?

A warm drug rolls through my veins, making me sleepy again, but just as I begin to drift, an actual person leans over me and cleans the goo from my eyes. Through the goo, I see a halo of red hair. *Rashiya.* My memory tugs at me. Tells me no. That can't be right.

The face is different.

Mom.

It's what my memories say when I see the face. The same angles and the same small green eyes that Rashiya had. But a leaner face, without the round, attractive apple cheeks of John Starfire, the crow's feet more visible around the eyes. No smile lines.

"You," she says, as the goo is cleaned from my face. "You bastard. Wake up. You've been saved, for whatever you're worth."

Feeling returns to my arms and legs, returning as pain, little needles pricking me in every pore all the way up my legs and arms. I remember this pain. From the first time I came out of a vat.

And then a warm flush, and I drift in and out as I'm cleaned off. I can't tell much of what is happening, save that I'm being moved to a bed. A clean bed in a bright room.

When I wake up, fog clouds the window, turning the room gray.

I sit up, and the gravity lacks any of the itch of the artificial stuff, and feels slightly off the Imperial standard. We're planetside. That's real weather out there. An ocean breeze, cold and moist and refreshingly salty, cuts through the house. It's not the cold, rainy shore where the Thuzerian city was. Grav feels nice and comfortable, if a bit light.

I look down at my body, naked under the cleanest sheets I've ever slept on. The synthskin job on my leg has been replaced by a much better one, the mesh under the skin so fine that there's no trace of it. I flex the leg and it feels as real as it used to, before I lost it. This is the kind of repair job only sentients can get.

I stand. The new leg feels good. Better than the last one. And my tongue . . . my tongue feels like it's all flesh as well.

I try speaking. "Salutes. Salutes."

No slur.

I look up and see Aranella.

She's sitting in a reclining chair, reading a book. She puts it down when she realizes I'm awake. And looks at me. Just looks, and calm as ever, says, "I'm Aranella."

I just avoid saying *I know*. She doesn't need to know I stole her daughter's memories in death. "You fixed my tongue." I don't slur it. "I thought it was unfixable."

"The vats have gotten better since we took over," she says. "Who knows more about crosses, a bunch of engineers, or crosses who have managed to outlive their projected lifespan?"

"Did you get rid of the . . ." I touch my face. The scars are still there.

"No, those I told the vat to leave. They suit you." She carefully folds a bookmark into the book and says, "Now, let's talk about why you attacked back there, and made yourself that much harder to find."

"Wait . . ." I say, and the last few hours return, if hazily. "You fired on us."

"I didn't fire. Someone in the Resistance did, yes." She lifts a soulsword—mine, I realize. Same soulsword I shoved through her daughter's heart. It catches what little light comes through the fog outside.

"I'd really like to shove this sword right through, suck up all your memories, the way you did to my daughter. And then it'll be over."

For half a second, I debate honesty or vulnerability. Honesty has always been overrated in war. "I didn't take Rashiya's memories," I lie. "I killed her. But it was a clean death."

She cocks her head, looks at me as if she can tell whether I'm lying. I hope I look convincing. I've never much needed to lie in my life. I've spent a lot more time delivering hard truth.

Her expression softens, just a hair.

"How long did you have me in a vat?"

"Two days. It took a little while to find you in that wreckage, but we followed the signature of the resonator in your sword."

"How long have I been out?"

"Long enough," she says. "Long enough for everything to change."

"What does that mean?"

No answer.

A non-sentient construct appears in the door. I've only seen them in holos, about rich bluebloods who have enough money to use such things. This one is featureless save for a few breathing holes at the neck. And creepy in person. You can hear it breathing. It has a particular smell too, a thick, sweet gel smell that I associate with the vats. A smell that, until a moment ago, I would have associated entirely with my friends.

"This is what a non-sentient being looks like," Aranella says. "Too bad they don't make good soldiers. We'd all be happier."

"You're using constructs? The Resistance is using constructs?"

"This planet has always used constructs. Where do you think you are?"

"Back on Irithessa?" I don't say that, if it weren't for her, I would figure I was in the afterlife.

"No. We realized quickly that Irithessa had to remain much the same way that it was. All that bureaucracy keeps things from falling apart, even in the midst of consolidation. They keep collecting taxes, they keep up maintenance on terraforming and make sure all the proper bribes are paid at unsavory nodes."

"No Directive Zero for the bureaucrats?"

"The bureaucrats know how lucky they are. The only humans in the galaxy who don't have to look over their shoulders."

The construct reaches out with a padded hand, helps me walk to a closet where a nice arrangement of normal street clothes waits for me. Trousers and shirts, hats and kilts. The kind of thing humans wear. I've never worn such innocuous clothes. Even on Shadow Sun Seven I dressed as a fighter. It dresses me up and I can't help thinking I look like the kid I never was.

Why is Aranella treating her daughter's murderer like this?

After I'm dressed, carefully moving the new leg, the construct turns me to face Aranella.

"You owe me now, Araskar. I wanted to leave you in space. More than that, I wanted to make a skewer of you, same as you did to my daughter. But I need you. So you're going to tell me everything you can about the girl. This new Son of Stars you've picked to replace my husband."

Jaqi. She knows about Jaqi?

"I don't ..."

"I need you. I hate it, but I do. And I need those kneelers and their masks."

"What?" I cough, and a bit of vat-juice spatters the bed. "Why? Why do you need us?"

She doesn't answer.

This business of asking questions with no answers is getting tiresome.

The construct leads me through the hallways of a house nicer than any I've ever been in. I see a piano, a massive thing that takes up half a room. More constructs working in the kitchen. Their cybernetic implants, delivering occasional data dumps, flicker with green light. The smell of frying onions and eggs drifts from the kitchen. My stomach groans, and I nearly bend double with hunger.

The construct leads myself and Aranella on a balcony, for the kind of view that sentients usually pay good money for.

Wherever we are, it is a paradise. A rocky beach stretches a few hundred feet below the balcony, and wisps of fog cling to the water and the oak-dotted hills around us, just burning off in the morning sunlight. The sun peeks through the fog out on the water.

"This is gorgeous," I say, and look over at Aranella. "I

could think I was dead, if you weren't here."

She narrows her eyes. It's too close to what Rashiya last said to her. They didn't part well—the memories are clear on that. Again, Rashiya's words run through my head. *Just find the person who killed me and throw them out an airlock.*

I could make my lie true. On the moon of Trace, I wanted to get rid of Rashiya's memories. I still can. Stick my small soulsword in my arm, suck them up, erase them handily, as I was trained to do with any battle trauma.

But those memories, right now, tell me how to deal with Aranella. The intel in them is priceless to the Reckoning. I hate myself for it, but I can't cleanse Rashiya from my mind, not yet.

For now, I'll hope Aranella continues to believe the lie.

"This is Keil," Aranella said. "You're standing on the same balcony where Formoz used to greet the morning."

I peer up at the sky, but it's too foggy to see the moons this morning, the moons where I almost got killed. "You know, I've actually met the children you stole this house from. They may be rich, but they didn't deserve what you did to them."

"We didn't steal the house from anyone," Aranella snaps. "They stole all their wealth, from the dead. From a thousand years of crosses going to be ground into meat in the Dark Zone."

I don't answer that.

"I'm going to ask you to come with me today, Araskar. I'm going to show you what the Resistance made, and see how our most high-profile traitor feels about it."

"I'm not your highest-profile traitor," I say. "It's you, isn't it? You're the leak in the Resistance."

She doesn't answer.

"Whatever you've made here, it can't last," I finally say.

"After you see what we've made, we'll talk. My husband's gone mad, and as much as I hate it, I need you, Araskar. I need to know about this girl."

"You think—" I stop myself from saying Jaqi's name. "You think the girl's the Son of Stars? You doubt your husband?"

"I don't know if there is a Son of Stars, or if it's just nonsense. But my husband's gone mad. He was mad when he ordered Directive Zero, and he's just gotten worse. He's also disappeared. And since he disappeared, the Shir have attacked three separate star systems."

It takes a long time to find the words for that, and when I do, they're stupid words to boot. "Oh. So that's what you meant when you said everything's changed."

Z

"Save the data!"

The Suits' cry goes through the city, the atmos, the entire planet. It goes through me, the nano-Suits in my bloodstream echoing the cry, rattling my nerves and screaming in my tendons.

My ship rears up, reaches for the sky, the thrusters roaring, burning unthunium. I am joined by the entire Suits' city. Towers and buildings and vast metal landscapes join together, twist and turn and form and re-form into massive ships, larger than any dreadnoughts, larger than some planets, tearing away from the planet's crust, leaving gaping holes and sending massive earthquakes through the planet—

It does not matter.

The planet is damned.

A black thread takes up the whole of the horizon. The finger of a dark god. The planet roars in pain as Abaddon pierces it. Dust clouds choke the air. Hurricane winds slam into my ship. The Suits bought sentient slaves to keep on this planet, grew bodies in vats, and so it has oceans, weather, air currents—none of them prepared to deal with the piercing, planet-killing touch of the Spider.

The data. I cannot tell, anymore, whether I hear the Engineer inside myself or inside the ship; all my efforts are to keep my ship from being tossed. Circuits and machinery and even what few plants remain on this planet are uprooted and tossed against my ship with the rush of the wind, the surge of the dust as crust and mantle are vaporized, as superdense Shir eggs implant on the inside of the planet.

I must reach the node. My thrusters burn and scream, the unthunium chamber roaring. I push it harder, for a better burn. Thrust, against gravity, shoves me hard against my seat. I fear that my ship, despite its sense-fields and its atmospheric protection, will be torn apart.

"Take the data!"

The voices come from inside me. The voices of a whole world of Suits, seeking to escape their fate.

My ship hurtles toward the upper atmosphere, carried on the storm. The metal screams. The heat shields wail. The sense-field begins to fail. Atmos hisses away from the ship, but I know I can survive for some time without it, so I do not concern myself.

And then, at last, I rise above the atmosphere of Trace. Below me, the world is all red lightning, black clouds, and death.

Suit ships, like whole moving cities, tear themselves out of the wrack one at a time. Massive clumps of circuitry, of towers joined together. They strive for orbit.

Too many fall back to the planet, caught by the roar of

lightning, the suck of the black thread.

I can still hear the Engineer, now joined with one of the ships. Take the data!

"Do you speak to me?" Almost as if I hear him through the dishonorable creatures implanted inside me.

You who know the purpose of the data. Take it.

I know not what he means. Take it? How? And does he mean all of his data?

My sensors register hostiles. Suits? Do they dare attack me now? Where are the—

Ah.

Superdense, light-absorbing, only illuminated by a few ultraviolet frequencies that must be translated by the sensors into a shape for my naked eyes. The Suits dishonorably implanted in my body aid in my perception. For I see *them*.

The Great Spiders.

Three of Abaddon, each larger than a star. Inside their vast bellies, stars still burn, eaten for fuel to power their massive bodies.

It is a mothering triad, the nightmare of every creature alive. Their black carapaces span vast gulfs of space, and their thousand legs twitch and glow with the strange energy that is their weapon—and their faces. By my ancestors, their faces, massive and alien, thousands of eyes. Jaws like broken spars that can swallow planets.

They only allow themselves to be seen on sensors when they are ready to kill—the rest of the time, they move faster than light, in the web of their own dark nodes.

And they are ready to kill.

One looms over the planet. Sickly blue light, like rotting vegetation, gathers at the ends of its thousand legs. It spirals and twists and forms a shape like a web—and it lays like a skein around the planet, to contain the Suits, keep them from escaping.

I increase thrust. The node is not far. Sensors tell me the Matakas have left the moon and are attacking the Shir.

They die in one twist of the blue energy, the web wrapping their ships and tearing through metal.

They died in something like honor.

I fear I will not.

The Engineer loses a piece of himself, and another. I do not need to pull it up on my sensors. I can see it in my head clearly. His ship was, when it first lifted off, miles and miles long, a moving city transforming itself into a vast dreadnought. Now it is little more than a single blade, stabbing for the freedom of the node. Daggers of sickly blue strike out, and where they touch, metal crumbles, circuits fail, and the Engineer loses data, his ship stripped, dying.

A thousand years he guarded that knowledge, and now he died.

I did not choose to be a vessel for the Suits, but I know this. The knowledge of my ancestors is most sacred above all. And in their own way, this the Suits appreciate.

I think a thing that they will be sure to hear. <u>Give me the data. And let me return to Jaqi.</u>

The Engineer's knowledge flows into me. The nano-Suits inside me suck up the data, their collective quantum memory taxed to organize that massive stream of information. Over a thousand years of data, since the first Suit attempted to bridge between the failed automatons of the First Empire and flesh sentience.

The Engineer's ship breaks apart—and three massive shards, glowing red and vile, planet-cracking shards, soar up from what was the Engineer's ship and tear through the Shir's web of energy, making a hole for my ship.

I burn through the rest of the fuel as my ship screams for the node.

The shards hit the attacking Spider. A vibration passes through my every molecule, a scream of something so massive it bends spacetime. More blue-white threads reach to weave a skein, trying to trap me—

Just as I pass through, before they close and the Suits die.

I escape the web of death, only because my ship's

thrust is far beyond safe levels for any sentient. I should be torn to pieces, my flesh jelly across my cockpit. But the Suits inside me hold me together.

The Great Spiders spin filaments of sickly blue, flying across the void for me, but I burn hard to the node.

In my head, a thousand years live and die, stories, songs, people long gone and long changed. It is the knowledge that the Suits have managed to put into me, though it is only a fragment of what they gathered. My mind cannot retain it—the entire Second Empire flashes through my poor brain and is forgotten. Dark nodes, the Imperial salvage, the worlds and people and stories that they have gathered, all the Engineer's knowledge, and then it is all gone.

But one piece of data sticks out, like a scream, like a battle cry, like the last words of the Engineer.

The Shir sing.

12

Jaqi

I BACK UP, TRYING not to trip. Those intense blue eyes are like shards burning me. I remember all the folk he's killed, and know I won't be but one more piece of meat on a sword.

"Whirr, you got any information on swordfighting?"

"Please state the style of swordfighting you prefer."

"The kind where you kill the other fella."

"The Earth-Mars Alliance forbids death in the process of a duel."

"Shame, that," John Starfire says as he walks toward me. "I'm going to take my memories back now."

"Whirr, I need you to shoot him. This man is dangerous," I say.

"That is not a proper command for my model," Whirr replies.

Worth a try.

I back up, between the pillars, and he comes for me. I hold Taltus's sword out like an idiot, like it's going to stop anything, and he holds his own sword up, in that way that tells me he really knows how to use it.

Being some Oogie of Stars won't help you, Jaqi. Got to use your head for one time in your life.

I've got this fella's memories, but none of the ones running through my head seem to relate to swordfighting.

"I know the secrets," I say. "I heard it here. It was humans done it to themselves. There weren't no Jorians. They was just humans what had special powers of the mind, and the devil was the creatures in pure space." I say it. "Shir—that just means Starfire. You can't kill all humans. We are all humans."

When I say it, the music flares up inside me, a distant song of the stars, moving through my blood. It *feels* true. We look at what the Jorians made—nodes and relay-towers and we figure it had to be some kind of miracle by a super-race, but it en't, it's just folk getting clever.

His face twists, and he laughs. "You believe that old lie?"

"That automaton done told me," I say. I'm trying to move faster, and my body reminds me of how much pain it's in as I do so. "Read it right from the records."

"A lot of old lies here," he says. "I'd like to go through them all, but I think we're better off without those ideas." He waves his sword. "It was a blessing in disguise when the Shir destroyed the library worlds. Think of how we'll start afresh."

This is a big room, but I'm still going to come up on a wall eventually, as I keep backing up. And there's no way out of here. Nothing. Unless I can pull yet another miracle.

The last miracle weren't nothing but a node. Nodes. What did I do back at Shadow Sun Seven? I was thinking about how I didn't want no one else to die—well, en't no one here but me, and I suspect I might be too foolish to live.

I was thinking about when I shot gray girl, Araskar's old lover, when this all started on Swiney Niney. Reached out for a node. Can I reach out for this one?

I try, but that's when John Starfire moves in and thrusts with his sword, and I try to bang it away, and he's strong and presses the attack and I stumble backward, and fetch up against one of the pillars, and he's slashed my leg open now—

Help me! I think of that thing I saw earlier. What appeared as my parents, then as a devil, but made of music.

I try to think of music. Try to think of my folks. But John Starfire's memories crowd it, full of fighting and blood—no, I need my mother's music, come on, where's the song—

I barely knock his sword aside, and he twists and punches me in the face, knocking me against the pillar.

But with that pain comes the hint of a song.

Bend, pull, bend, pull . . . till the wheelbarrow's full.

My mother's voice.

And then an answering voice, from the Starfire itself.

<u>Bend, pull, bend, pull . . . till the wheelbarrow's full.</u>

A torrent of music pours into me from the universe around, drenches me, drowns me—

John Starfire leaps suddenly, his blade coming for me.

But I en't there no more.

With a scream and a yank, I go flying across untold pure space. A rush like I never felt, a feeling like my body's spread across the eternities.

And I'm back, standing on the bridge on the temple of the planet in the center of the Dark Zone.

I fall on my knees, clutch the railing. I feel like my insides all been wrung out. Aw hell. Aw hell. I just went between galaxies like it weren't no thing.

This business of doing miracles is wearing me out.

The temple walls stretch high around me. Now that I've seen it, I reckon this place was supposed to be a mate to that Archives Tower back in orbit around Earth. If they was going to fill it with archived information filling up the pillars, they never built no pillars.

Far as I can tell, down below this bridge there's only seawater.

All that information's still back there, in orbit around Earth. With John Starfire wanting to smash it. I don't read none, but if there's one thing I've learned today, it's that we could all use more stories about what happened when the First Empire went out the airlock.

"You there?" I ask the empty space. Looking for that thing—that creature made of music.

It hits me like some planet-sized echo of my mother's song. I can feel her so close in the music I can almost taste it. Tapping her hips against the counter, and singing while she cuts a tomato.

And I see that thing. Well, *see* en't the right word for it, but I know it's there.

"So you's what the devil was originally."

Again, I'm translating from the thoughts that come into my head with a rush of music, so forgive me, cuz this en't quite it, just the closest it can be in words. <u>We are not like you. We are not part of time, part of fixed space. Those who came before . . . they were in pain and they sought to exist in fixed space, to aid those they loved. It . . . changed them. They tried to go into the corrupted space, and they were themselves corrupted.</u> There is a sadness to the music, a kind of bad feeling running through it. <u>They saw the ones they loved being hurt,</u>

changed. They themselves were hurt, changed. They feel only hunger now.

"So your . . . ancestors? They were in pain?"

The music strikes a couple of quirky notes. It don't know the word *ancestors*. Okay, worth a try.

"Them . . ." I make myself say it. "Them . . . Shir that lived in pure space, back before they was—monsterized." Okay, that en't a word, but for someone who en't a book bug, I'm doing the best I can. "Why was they in pain?"

It comes to me, like it's a story being told through song.

A virus, John Starfire was right. Only, he was half right. He thinks it was a virus humans made to kill Jorians, but I know that en't right now. It was a nasty thing, a microbe that got turned fearsome during terraforming. I've seen plenty of that, out in the spaceways—you hear tell of planets that should support sentient life just fine, but something is wrong in the soil, in the air, some bug kills everything that comes down there.

I almost see it.

An empire that spread across galaxies died. All them folk, their skin turning red from broken blood vessels, hacking blood into their hands. It was a long, painful death, and the music, representing it, turns chaotic, mad, like an orchestra sawing away at their instruments fit to smash them. I see the First Empire falling. Whole star systems just stopped talking on the node-relays. Whole galaxies. With trade so connected by the nodes, the virus could get anywhere. Planets only survived by cutting off their nodes, when they could.

In those days each ship had a navigator, a person who could follow the nodes, connected to a creature of pure space. These things that existed in a different dimension, but they was as connected, surely as Scurv is connected to vir guns. They was—what's that word—symbionts.

And so the Shir in pure space felt every single death from that disease, and it drove them into some kind of madness. I sense it, as much as anyone can. A whole host of them as became the devil, mad from the pain, the music turned into splintering, jigsawing roars. So they threw themselves against the nodes they had made, and they shifted dimensions, came into our space, where they was never meant to be.

And they changed.

Went from being creatures of pure space to being the devils.

And, I reckon, the only piece of alien life in the universe that en't crossed with humans.

I need to get to my feet. Need to get out there, outside this temple, find Scurv, bring vim back and send vim through the node to shoot John Starfire for good.

The music presses on me of a sudden. I'm not sure what it's saying, but this thing don't want me to leave. <u>I must bond,</u> it "says." It en't quite *bond,* either—it's almost a combination of *bond* and *become* and a bunch of other feelings what relate to changing.

"What you talking about?"

Someone with a better brain could say this in a way that makes sense, but this is mostly what it tells me: <u>I am adult. I must bond. I reached for you, but the other was here first, and I cannot bond if he is strong. He bent me to his will, to make him travel. He can again.</u>

"So . . . you want to bond with me, the way you done with the ancients . . ." Whatever you call them. "But John Starfire is in the way?"

<u>His reach is strong. His call is strong. I do not feel the bond</u>—becoming, growing, it's more than *bond,* but that's the best my puny brain can do when it's told something through music—<u>with he as I do with you, but he seeks it. You must stop him from reaching out, or we will not unify.</u>

Even this thing reckons I'm some Chosen Oogie. "How am I supposed to beat a fella took down the entire galaxy?"

The music swells, rises up around me, as if it's telling me <u>I am with you.</u>

Well, I reckon that's almost a vote of confidence.

Course, as much as it's great to have the real living Starfire itself on my side, this is a fella who took down a galactic empire.

But a plan starts to form in my head. Guess my evil small brain has grown a few sizes lately.

"Send me back to Earth's moon. Let's kill John Starfire."

13

Araskar

WE TAKE A HOVERBUG from Formoz's seaside manor along a line of cliffs to a place where the coast opens up. Below, the long spread of sand is dotted with people. Young people. Lots of young adults, in their prime. I see only a couple of children.

"You're about to live the dream, Araskar," Aranella says.

I don't answer. *Three star systems.*

There's no words.

The hoverbug comes in for a landing at a public platform. The guy waving us to our parking spot has my face. The market is bright with colors, bright with fabrics and signs written both in Imperial standard and a language I don't recognize. People move along laughing, chatting with each other. And when I say *people,* I mean crosses.

A sea of the same eighteen faces, those used again and again for the military models. My own face repeats about a dozen times, as do the faces of my slugs—Helthizor and Joskiya—and my friends, Barathuin and Karalla, everyone I've lost. Over and over again, the same faces, with different arrangements of scars. A few unique faces—probably from agricultural crosses, or those outliers, like Jaqi, whose parents managed to reproduce—break up the monotony.

But I've never seen these faces without a uniform. I've seen them over and over again in cramped ships, between Moths, over training swords and under emergency lights. I've never seen these faces smiling under a bright open sky, wearing loose, casual clothes, looking like they've taken a long lunch to enjoy the sunshine. That's the kind of thing humans do. Humans get weathered skin from real sunlight. Humans laugh and sit out on cafes drinking coffee with a touch of thurkuk. Humans talk about politics like those politics don't get us killed.

And humans have children. It seems like every third woman I see is pregnant. A whole new batch of crosses, being cooked up at home just like John Starfire promised.

Over and over. Not wearing military uniforms. Scars on plenty of them. Synthskin shining through the netting that merges it with regular skin. Most of these are veterans, I'm sure.

"Welcome to the dream," Aranella says, co-opting my thoughts. "Can you quote it?"

"If you mean the actual book itself, no," I say. John Starfire's book, *Toward a New Sentience*, was supposed to be required reading in the Resistance. Few of us actually read it, because he quoted it so much in the required-viewing holos. "I read *My Private Vat*."

"That one was written by a human," Aranella says, shaking her head. "An incrementalist, to make it worse. Ten years ago, when all we had was a handful of ships. Why is it that all of you read that one, and not John's book?"

"Sometimes you want to know what happened before."

"But he was a moderate." She's referring to the author of *My Private Vat*, the book credited with starting the cross-rights movement. "He thought that crosses should be allowed to retire from the army into society, but that the army must be maintained."

"Tell me, then," I say, turning to her face, her unique face in a crowd filled with my face and the faces of all my dead friends. "Do we need the army? Have you shut down the vats, as promised? Who is maintaining what's left of the Navy?"

She doesn't answer.

"What happens now? You can't fight the Shir with a bundle of happy citizens. You need all the vats, and all the forges, to be running at top speed." The words tumble out of me. "Three star systems."

In one of the strangest things that's ever happened, in any galaxy, Aranella doesn't answer. Instead, she walks five steps to a booth and buys me ice cream.

She hands me the flake-and-cream without a word.

Rashiya's memories bubble up. She's a child, taking ice cream from her mother's hand. *Crosses aren't allowed to have this,* child-Rashiya says, confused, and her mother laughs. *Your father pulled some strings.*

She meets my gaze and I look away.

The ice cream is amazing.

It's cold and sweet and perfect, with a hint of mango and strawberry under vanilla. I suspect there is actual real fruit and vanilla in it, not just a clever flavoring. I had plenty of ice cream during those training days in the Navy, but it was cheap, mass-produced stuff.

We end up on the beach, watching the waves. Crosses, many bearing the signs of synthskin and battle, run into the water. A couple are surfing. The few children, mostly infants and very young toddlers, sit on blankets and poke at the sand. Their parents try to stop the children from eating said sand.

It's all so normal, and I just want to scream *Three star systems!*

The signs are all new, with a second language underneath Imperial Standard. Even the ones that say *Mind the*

Lifeguards and *Stay Inside the Buoys*. I don't understand the second language, which is odd, considering how many languages came with my data dump. I keep waiting for recognition to hit, like it did with the Matakas and their nest queen, and it never does—the signs remain a mystery. "What is that?"

"The only language every cross has to learn the old-fashioned way. Our own language."

I can't help laughing. "You worry about that? Now? You know as well as I do that all this is a lie." I spread out my arms, and nearly drop my ice cream, which would be a terrible mistake, as it's cold and sweet and wonderful. "The Shir are free."

She exhales. "It's you who don't understand."

"What don't I understand? The vats are still operating, aren't they? They would have to be." It's so strange to have this discussion on a pleasant beach, surrounded by gorgeous, happy couples, eating the ice cream. It feels so far away. "For the Empire to exist, it must exist in a state of eternal war. There must be a soldier class. John was a fool to think otherwise."

"It's you who don't understand." Aranella takes a lick of her own ice cream. "John wants peace because he *wants* the Shir to reproduce."

That takes a minute. I stare at her, openmouthed, until the ice cream melts and runs out the side of my mouth.

"He—what?"

"He wants them to have children, and they need inhabited planets to do that. I confronted him, and he said they have to reproduce. Those were his words. Have to."

"Did he . . . explain why?" I'm still trying to wrap my head around this. Are the Shir controlling John Starfire somehow?

"He tried. It was nonsense." I think she's going to say more about this nonsense, but she doesn't. She turns and looks out at the ocean again. "I've seen the Imperial estimation of how many Shir are in the Dark Zone. They haven't produced a new generation in a millenium, the Navy has logged at least a thousand kills in just the last few years, and there are still billions of adult Shir in there. Imagine billions of mothering triads. Each one willing to crack a planet open for a full harvest of eggs."

It's actually making my head hurt more. I thought John Starfire was a misguided demagogue; he wanted to rule the galaxy and get rid of the humans. No, he's a devil-worshipper?

"So John told me something insane and vanished."

"When was this?"

"He vanished a week ago. Right after that, I told the fleet he was dead."

"The Resistance thinks John Starfire is dead?"

She nods. "Lots of crying. You wouldn't think hardened veterans could cry so hard."

"We have our sensitive moments."

"I told them we would accept the Thuzerians' offer to trade you for peace. I thought all was well, right up until someone fired back there. I didn't give the order to fire, Araskar. And now I can't trust any of my officers. I don't know which of them—maybe all of them—John's controlling."

"How many of them know about the Shir attack?"

"Rumors are flying. I can't order them to attack the Shir if they don't recognize my authority."

I can't think of what to say to that.

"I got rid of that memory crypt, sent it to Formoz, because I knew why John wanted it." You wouldn't think you'd ever hear someone incriminate herself as a traitor over ice cream on a beautiful day. "He thought it was the last piece of information he needed about the Dark Zone. He used to be so focused on the cause. And then . . ." She takes a long time for the next few words. "And then he became something else. Angry. Obsessed. Sleepless. Religious to boot. I shed no tears for the bluebloods, but killing every human in the galaxy? Do you know what it's like to hear those words come out of your husband's mouth? Do you know what it's like to see your *daughter* believe that idea?" She looks at me again, and laughs, without humor. "Of course you don't."

Aranella Starfire. Perhaps the least likely ally in all the worlds, but she knows everything we need to use against her husband.

Aranella Starfire. My best ally in this war. Except I killed her daughter.

She takes a bite of the flaky crust wrapped around the ice cream. "He promised me we would be safe. All of us safe. I didn't know that meant that he was giving the Shir the wild worlds to eat."

We are both silent, eating ice cream that has lost a bit of its sweetness, watching a scene we never thought to see.

A good couple platoons' worth of people are playing in the water of a beach they took from bluebloods. And I'm thinking about billions more Shir. A Dark Zone that'll stretch three times the size of its current length. And crosses. We'll need trillions of crosses to fight them off. We'll need all the vats plus more. And if John Starfire comes back from wherever he went, he'll have these troops. I knew this was coming, but like a fool, I thought I had time.

"I'm not convinced we need a Chosen One," Aranella says. "Any Chosen One. But I need the kneelers' ships. I'll take your messiah over mine if it gets me Thuzerian dreadnoughts."

"You don't need Jaqi. You need me."

"I know." She pulls a terminal comm from her pocket. "I don't have access to the node-relay right now. My First-blade says it's a technical problem. Says to visit the central node-relay here in the city. My ship is in orbit, but all my subordinates seem to think it's a great idea for me to relax on the planet's surface."

"You're cut off."

"I don't think I would last an Imperial minute on that bridge." She walks back toward where we parked. "I need you to speak to the Thuzerians, which means hijacking a node-relay to send a message that will broadcast my treachery loud and clear."

"S'funny." I finish my ice cream, and seriously wonder if I have any money in my account to go back for more, before I remember my account is probably frozen.

"What's funny about this situation?"

"Everything." I try to fix her with her gaze, not let her see what she's done to me. "Everything you and your husband said. We were made for more than to just die in the Dark Zone. Now, here we are, making plans to die in the Dark Zone."

I think she's going to snap again. No. Just more words. "I believed him. You couldn't help believing him, before . . ." I hear the unspoken words. *Directive Zero.* "It's why I started a family. John went into the Dark Zone and came out alive, with word that the Shir were going to hold to a cease-fire. It was an unbelievable claim, but everything he did was unbelievable. I believed him."

Right then, we pass someone plunking away at a guitar, sitting in the sand. And I'm reminded of the first night on the moon of Trace, when I looked at the guitar Jaqi went to a lot of trouble to save.

And I feel a strange urge, a need to make peace. Not a familiar feeling. But one I felt when I held that guitar, and when I thought of whole soaring songs and unembodied suites I needed to play.

"This is going to sound strange."

"Because today's been a normal day?"

"I want to ask your forgiveness."

"What?"

"Call me bizarre, or broken, or gone in the head." I think I'm probably all three. "I would like to ask your forgiveness for what I did to Rashiya."

"You're saying you're sorry?" She spits out the words. "You're sorry that you murdered my daughter?"

"Of course I'm sorry," I say. "I don't regret why I did it, but I sorrow. If I'm going to die fighting the Shir, I would welcome your forgiveness."

I can't help thinking of Jaqi. Of the way it felt to wake up next to her and truly want to keep living.

Here I am, Barathuin, Helthizor, even Rashiya, all my dead friends. Here I am without you, and I still want to go on. More than that, I want to go on into a life of peace. I don't want to chew on my anger, my loneliness, any more than I want to chew on pills.

"Forgiveness." She shakes her head. "You ask for my forgiveness."

And then she kicks me right between the legs, and I fall to the ground, in blinding pain.

I must be getting used to blinding pain, though, because I still make out what she says, half muttered as it is. "I thought you couldn't hurt me anymore."

14

Araskar

I SAID I WOULD never wear the uniform of the Vanguard again, and here I am in a fresh pair of fatigues, walking down the well-lit hall of an Imperial communications complex, past various Imperial symbols scratched and scrubbed out and occasionally covered up with Resistance decals. I half expect Rashiya to materialize at my side—in real life—again. It feels like I'm back on drugs.

It's what it takes to get Aranella through the halls. She needs a normal-looking cross soldier with her, since she's managed to ditch her assigned bodyguards.

"Come on," she says, irritated at my slowness.

"I'm trying." My body needs more rest, having been pulled from that vat as soon as the work was done. "Still healing up here. That kick didn't help."

We pass through another hallway, past a batch of joking crosses who stop and salute Aranella. I would think they would recognize my face, but they must assume I'm just another cross, maybe wounded.

"Didn't you stick my face up everywhere?" I say, when yet another cross walks by with barely a look. "The Kurguls had an image of me."

"We had to take it down," she said. "There are lots of crosses with your face and a few scars. Half the Resistance turned themselves in."

Well, that's one good thing about sharing a face with a billion other people.

We reach the main node-relay room. Unlike the one I hacked back on the moon of Trace, this is a properly maintained node-relay, sending and receiving tens of thousands of faster-than-light messages each hour. Banks of knobs and lights and wires rise high above our heads in each direction.

"Regent!" A cross, with the same face as Joskiya, jumps up from her seat. "I didn't know you were coming."

"I need to get a message through," Aranella says.

"Of course, Regent. I can patch you in through the fleet—"

"Not the fleet." Aranella steps forward. "What's your name?"

"I... I haven't decided." The communications tech seems flustered. "It didn't seem right to focus on a name when there was, ah, so much going on. But I'm leaning toward Dinetrifi."

"Dinetrifi. A warrior queen, from just before Joria

even expanded into space. John took his own Jorian name from that era, you know. Jaceren, the king who launched the first ships into the nodes."

"Yes," she says, looking everywhere but at Aranella. "The Regent's name. I don't say it, of course."

"I will miss him dearly," Aranella says, staring right at the girl.

"We all will," she replies, looking everywhere except at Aranella.

I watch the cross's face carefully. This girl doesn't believe John Starfire's dead. Aranella wasn't kidding.

"Just give me control of a node-relay, and we'll be on our way."

She does so, leading Aranella to one of the big monitors among the wires and knobs, and hardly gives me a second glance—but this girl is nervous.

Thing about being a soldier—you train so you won't be nervous. You shoot and swing a sword enough times, the training takes over. But you're not trained how to deal with a conflict in your orders. When your orders don't make any sense, then it's clear the higher-ups don't care about the troops in the field.

And so I put one hand on my short soulsword, and draw it very slowly, as quietly as I can, tuck it up into the crook of my arm.

"Do you have the frequency? I should really—"

"I'll input the frequency myself," Aranella says.

"Oh, but I'll have to transmit the clearance code."

Aranella speaks through gritted teeth. "Tell me the clearance code."

Poor little no-name communications officer, possibly to be called Dinetrifi, possibly to be dead if she irritates Aranella.

And Aranella is wearing a soulsword—the easiest way to just take the knowledge from her mind anyway.

"Give her the clearance code," I say, making my tone clear.

To-be-Dinetrifi mutters, "Five-nexus-seven-mercury-nine."

"Thank you." Aranella sits down and begins hard-encoding the frequency and the clearance code both, a process that requires a lot of knob-twisting and button-pushing, a process, I'm guessing, that is designed to be confusing to anyone but a trained communications officer.

"It's transmitting," Aranella says to me, and leans in and whispers, "The Thuzerian Council is going to get my request."

Let's hope they don't take too long to call back.

And right on cue, there are footfalls. Running soldier feet, echoing down the corridor.

Aranella stands up, looks at me. "Are you going to try and hide yourself?"

"Not exactly," I say.

Here they are, led by me.

My face, though with only one scar instead of the jigsaw I bear. This one's wearing the Secondblade insignia, my old insignia that I left at Trace.

"Kineroth," Aranella says to the new arrival, who has brought a whole squad with him. "Thought you were in orbit."

"I know who this is," Secondblade Kineroth says, his face twisting in anger. "The Regent is dead, you said?"

Aranella doesn't answer.

"Shortly after you told us he had died, we got an encrypted message from the dead Regent."

"Let me guess," she says. "He ordered you to attack the Thuzerians, against my orders to accept the prisoner transaction."

Kineroth raises his soulsword. Several emotions war in his face, as if he's trying to find a way to explain Aranella's behavior to himself. "The Regent's consort is confused. She is not making sense." He glares at me, a kind of hilarious expression with that babyface. "And this one—"

He can't say what he wants to about me, because Aranella draws her soulsword faster than I'd thought possible and attacks.

Aranella isn't the swordsman that any trained soldier

is, though, and that becomes clear a second later when Kineroth disarms her, and she falls backward, against me, and turns and looks at me—

And I put my sword up to her neck. "Sorry," I say. "The Regent has one more agent here."

"What?" Aranella says.

"What?" the Secondblade says.

"It's true," I say, hoping that both Aranella gets it, I sound convincing, and I don't drop the sword, because shit, does it feel heavy. I should have had more ice cream before I took another stupid risk. "I was the Regent's agent from the beginning, investigating the rival Chosen One."

"That's insane," the one named Kineroth says. "Drop the sword, before I—"

"That would be how I know about Black Martha."

"What the hell is Black Martha?"

Everyone looks confused, except for one of the soldiers standing behind Secondblade Kineroth. She is looking at me as though I've just grown another head. And while I stand there she steps up, and says something, and Kineroth the Secondblade's face contorts. "You're black ops."

Black Martha was the nickname Rashiya and a few of her compatriots gave to the memory-crypt only they had access to. It's a long shot, in this case, but just about everything has been so far.

I try to sound very calm. I think that being tired helps. I don't think I've ever lied so totally in my life. "I'm black ops. I infiltrated the Reckoning, and extorted a promise of help from the Thuzerians. "

And for a moment I catch a glimpse of Aranella's face.

As she realizes that I lied about taking her daughter's memories.

For the first time, I see what Rashiya saw so often—Aranella, knowing that she's been betrayed.

"Come with us," Kineroth says.

"Yes, sir," I say. "Interrogation?"

"No time for that. Maybe you can shed some light on what the hell we're supposed to do about the Shir."

———

Jaqi

Back through the node to Earth that was lost. Back to face John Starfire.

I stagger and nearly fall over—and it's a damn good thing I don't, because my musical friend en't sent me back to the floor of the Archives Tower.

No, I'm on a catwalk about a thousand feet up. A

spindly, thin catwalk, barely big enough for both of my feet, going from one archive pillar to another.

There's a whole web of these catwalks, going from pillar to pillar up here, but I don't so much pay attention to them as I do the dizzy sight of them pillars, stretching an evil way down to the floor, and a speck on that floor I think is Whirr.

And I puke, all the decent food left in me, watch it sail all the way to the floor of this Archives Tower.

Takes a good long time to get down there. Any other time, I would have been highly entertained by such a thing. At least the gravity in this spot is light, the field having given out. If I fall, I won't fall too fast.

I catch my breath, gasp, and look up.

There's John Starfire, on the same catwalk.

It's dark up here, so only the white light of his soulsword illuminates his face—all them smile lines and the scars and the hairs of his beard in bright white light.

"So you've talked to it. You think I haven't?"

<u>Okay,</u> I say to the thing made of music—the uncorrupted devil—<u>I wanted you to send me back with a bit of an advantage!</u> Except the moment I think it, the dull blue light along my soulsword flickers and starts to go out. I stop thinking about that, and try madly to think, evil loud:

I can do this. I can beat this bastard. Said to myself, not to anything else.

The blue fire comes back, feeding off my faith in myself.

"You think I can't see how you did it?" he asks. "I can. I saw you make the node and jump here, and I followed you. I saw what you just did. You're moving the original node, the one from the planet in the Dark Zone to here. It goes wherever you go. It's tricky, but I can figure it out."

"Yeah, yeah, yeah," I say. "Did you conquer the Emperor with talking?"

The flame on my blade burns brighter. Seems it works off faith and mouth both. Evil good for me. I en't much for faith, but I got plenty of mouth.

He comes at me and I again make just a pathetic slash to knock his sword away, barely keeping him from carving me to bits. I slide my feet backward, feeling my way along this catwalk.

"You don't understand, do you?" he says. "I see what makes you special now, and that means I can do it."

"Lots of creeps spied on me. Happens in the spaceways. Don't mean you learned everything."

He rushes forward, trying to use the light gravity to his advantage, throw me back. I'm too busy trying to back up along the catwalk, keep my balance, and slide my feet back and back—so he gets me, knocks my sword aside, and cuts a slice right out of my right breast. I jerk backward—

Right into Imperial standard gravity. I nearly fall, just catch myself. Suddenly my balance is a hell of a lot harder to maintain. Burning art-grav!

The music swells and I reach out and think, <u>Get me an advantage</u> and—

I *shift,* but unlike taking a node from one galaxy to the other, this is hardly a shift at all—except that now I'm on a different catwalk, another spider-web thin thing all the higher than the last one, looking down at John Starfire. I even forget about the blood rushing down my chest for a moment.

"Ha!" I shout down.

And then, "Oh shit."

He twists, and just as sharp as if he'd stabbed me again, here he is, coming through the mini-node I've just used. His bright sword appears first, and then the rest of him appears from the air.

So this is what the uncorrupted devil meant. He can use all that same magic I can.

He comes at me again—but he staggers, like he's drunk, grits his teeth. I raise my sword. Blood trickles into the waist of my pants. But he's been hurt too. "It don't work for you like it do for me," I say. "That thing—the creature of Starfire—it don't like you, do it?"

"Pain never stopped me before." He rushes me and I try to smack away the soulsword blows, ignore the way that moving tears the rip in my breast all the more.

"Not everyone loves you, handsome," I say. "Bet that just keeps you up nights."

His face contorts and he growls, "You're just a loose end. Just more consolidation."

There's another catwalk within jumping distance. But the gravity's Imperial standard here, and were I anyone with sense, I wouldn't try it.

I'll never match this fella in a swordfight, so I jump.

And land, and my feet slip out, and I grab at the catwalk, and start to fall—

"Aiya!" I reach out for the music and twist through a node—

And land on another catwalk, even higher.

Low grav again. Phew.

This is getting interesting. Okay, Jaqi, you got your own private node here and it obeys you real nice. Can you tell it not to let him through?

I can't think how. It'd take years to get skill with this.

The huge central reactor at the top of these pillars is humming along, pulsing blue light. Must be one of the first things folk built to be powered by solar power and space radiation, and them automatons have kept it in shape all these years.

Looking down, I see John Starfire jump from one catwalk to another, and twist, and vanish, and—

I turn and stab at the empty air in front of me.

And he appears behind me. Shit. I run along the catwalk, and he chases me. This particular spindly little catwalk won't get me much of anywhere; it dead-ends into one of the pillars, and it's harder to stop in this low grav—I slide a good long ways along the catwalk after I put my feet down. The sound of me sliding echoes among the big empty space all around the pillars. I turn and face him, see the pain on his face, and I reach out to the music again. It sweeps through me. My mother's voice, big as all of space, singing.

<u>Bend, pull, bend, pull, pick the cotton, shear the wool, go until the wheelbarrow's full.</u>

I jump through the node again.

I'm high as I can go, and back in high gravity again, ready to pull me to a splatter on the floor. Just below the main reactor now. The blue light washes out the blue flame of my sword. Can't risk any more blind jumps, as they just seem to be taking me a little bit higher, unless I can figure out how to go lower.

I reckon I en't got time to figure anything out. You gotta win this swordfight, Jaqi, or die.

Here he comes. In front of me, but a little farther away this time, he materializes, a good two feet away from the catwalk, out in open air—

And before he's finished, before he can fall, he just *leaps* right over to the catwalk.

Shit.

"You run. That's all you do. I don't run." He approaches me, sword out. "I've never run. That's why it'll be me, not you."

Okay, I say to the music, I reckon I got my head on straight here. This is the plan. I visualize what I want to do.

"You think the uncorrupted Shir is somehow magic," he says as he gets closer. "I know. You've heard stories of the Starfire, nonsense from Bible-pushers and bluebloods, and you think this is the incarnation of everything godly. But it's just an animal. It reaches out blindly."

The music fills me up. Once again, it's like I'm standing over Z with a sword. Like I'm on Shadow Sun Seven reaching out to save seven thousand folk. And like my mother is there, running her rough fingers through my hair while she sings.

I taste something familiar, as familiar as the music. Crisp and sweet, dusted with salt. A fresh tomato. Well, I'll be.

"There is no purpose to what it does, and no purpose to what the universe does." John Starfire comes closer.

"And when I take all your memories, it'll be happy with me as its bond."

He lunges.

I enter pure space—and I go right *through* him, turn around, and find myself facing his back.

And, not that it's sporting, but I stab him in the back.

15

John Starfire

YOU WOULD HAVE TO be an idiot not to be afraid. To stare at a wide expanse of starless space, the darkness full of the nightmares of a few trillion sentients?

He's afraid.

The fear sharpens the hope.

Not two hours ago, he stood in the Imperial Navy's central hub, examining supply lines. Dreadnoughts blinking in and out of the Dark Zone. Casualty numbers from a never-ending war against the Shir.

John Starfire pushed a few buttons, activated the clearance he'd taken from the Emperor's mind with his soulsword, and changed the node-codes. The pure-space relay pinged. Military node-codes were changed on a fairly regular basis anyway. This would have been routine, as long as the new codes had been communicated.

But they hadn't.

No one knew these new codes but him.

That quickly, and the lines of supply stopped. Not a

single dreadnought in the Dark Zone would ever leave. As soon as they ran out of ammunition, they'd be Shir food.

The only way they might escape would be if there was one of the very rare cases among them, one of the crosses born with an instinctive ability to manipulate nodes. But John Starfire looked all over the galaxy for one like that, and found no one.

Now, he stands before the Dark Zone.

Within those nightmarish light-years, that massive section of starless space, whole Imperial dreadnoughts are being torn apart. Billions of soldiers are dying, firing off their last planet-crackers and missiles. They will each be fighting the fear, trying to die with what little honor they thought they owed their masters. They will be swimming in vacuum. Looking for hope, like he once did.

He hates to think of it. They don't deserve to die. But he has done what he must.

He breathes in the stale, recycled air of his small ship.

He breathes in his own fear.

You don't need to be afraid, he tells himself. *You're it. You're the prophesied one, the Son of Stars.* It feels real, feels right, coming from his mouth. *The children are the key.* All he has to do is let the Shir bear one generation of young.

What if you're wrong?

He curses that voice. It's normally quiet, but two days

ago Aranella doubted him, and it's been all the stronger since.

"*Our daughter is in one of those units that'll make planetfall,*" *Aranella says.* "*On Irithessa. John, I can't think of her doing—*"

"*She made her choice, Nella.*"

"*No,*" *she says.* "*Formoz is right. If there is a chance to wind down the war slowly, with negotiation, we should take it. Think of how many troops will die when we attack Irithessa.*" *Aranella stands up.* "*Be patient this time.*"

"*I am speaking as the Son of Stars, Aranella.*"

She fixes him with her gaze, the words unsaid trembling on her lips. "*It cannot be that easy. You're speaking the words of God, just because you want to be right?*"

"*I know when it's destiny. I can taste it. I can see it all, laid out in front of me.*" *The words taste right. He can feel the truth on his lips.*

"*I don't believe you.*" *She puts a tender hand on his arm.* "*For one thing, you haven't slept in a week.*"

He yanks his arm away from her. "*You doubt me? Now? Just because our daughter is in danger?*"

"*I've always doubted you,*" *she says.* "*Someone has to.*"

"*Not anymore,*" *he snaps.*

"*If our daughter dies, Jaceren, I won't forget this.*"

"*She won't die,*" *he replies.* "*Trust me.*"

The big moments unroll before him. The Empire,

falling. The Shir, bearing more children.

Now, he enters the node. Punches in the code, vanishes into the darkness.

It's cold.

It's dark.

The cockpit is lit only by a sickly blue half-light, like rotting vegetation. Voices whisper, and he's chilled, and his fear all the stronger.

The fear speaks with his voice. *The humans know. They know what you're doing. They'll regroup, and then you'll never be rid of them. They'll get into everything. They'll make you serve. The humans. The humans.*

A fear even louder than the voices. *You are one of them. You are just a human, and Jorians are just a myth.*

And the voice he recognizes. *You aren't the Son of Stars. You're a cross who got lucky. The words feel right because you want them to be right.*

He grits his teeth against that one, against the way it tears into him.

And then a different voice, one as cold as vacuum. <u>You have no name.</u>

He doesn't know how they do that. "I have many names. You can call me Jaceren." He doesn't hesitate to use the Jorian name anymore, even if it's not the one that made him famous.

<u>You have no name.</u>

On the display, a million planet-sized threads shift, like a great web.

One of *them* is near.

He speaks, and the air in his ship tastes like an open grave.

He tries to keep the memories clear, everything that came through the memory-crypt. *The children are key.* The Shir's children.

"I came to offer you something."

<u>Offer. Us.</u>

There are others now. He doesn't know how he knows this, but he can sense them as well. They move through the dark webs, faster than light, yet restricted to the Dark Zone. Why? Because they have fallen from pure space?

"You've enjoyed this, yes? A Navy that you can beat for once. A battle that doesn't end with retreat."

<u>Retreat?</u> Pain floods him. They're angry now. Good, he tries to remind himself, it's good to make them angry. He can use their anger against them.

"I offer you time. World where you can implant your children." He doesn't pause, despite the importance of the phrase. "A cease-fire." Only for a few months, God, let it be so. The Empire must be consolidated, the blue-bloods removed, crosses installed in power, and then, most crucially of all, the Shir, who have not produced a new generation in a thousand years, must be allowed to produce one new generation of juveniles. And then all his Resistance will be restored to the full glory of the Jorians.

If it works.

It will work. He is the Son of Stars, and so it will work.

<u>You taste like fear. You taste like fury.</u>

<u>You taste like all things good.</u>

Their whispers sound like the fear. The sort of thing that lives at the back of his mind, trying to drag him into the darkness. Trying to keep him from what he knows to be true, that humans are a scourge, that he was chosen to eliminate the scourge. He is the Chosen One.

<u>You are the one, yes?</u>

And after a moment, the voices whisper, <u>No. No, you are not the one.</u>

He stops. "What?" They sound so much like the voice, the doubt that clamors at the back of his mind, that it takes a moment to recognize that they spoke again.

<u>You are not the one. The tenderest of flesh. That one is yet to come.</u>

"What are you . . ." Stop, he thinks, it makes no difference what the Shir babble about.

But fear seizes the back of his mind, a clutching, grasping, terrible fear. He must be the Son of Stars. If he is not chosen, if he is not going to find the legendary uncorrupted ones and make more nodes, if he cannot head a Third Empire—then all of it is in vain. All of it. He clutches his sword's hilt, shaking, half drawing it before he remembers a sword won't do any good.

<u>Your fear is sweet.</u>

He forces the words, against the fear. "A cease-fire. Will you take my offer?"

<u>What will you give us?</u>

"I am broadcasting, on a universal Imperial channel, the locations of solar systems you can attack without fearing reprisal." Death sentences to those solar systems. He hates himself for it. Trillions of innocents will die and it will be his fault. But there must be another generation of Shir.

<u>We can make our larvae there.</u>

"Are you speaking as the Son of Stars?" Aranella's words twist and pivot in his mind. They spin like webs.

He opens his mouth, to answer Aranella, and answers instead the devils. "Yes."

And a prayer, a desperate prayer escapes his lips. A weak, momentary prayer, to a God he thought he forgot.

"Let me be right."

———

Jaqi

I yank the sword from the bastard's back. Them devils' voices spin in my mind, crawl down my spine. The force of the yank sends me reeling backward, and the vast distance below us yawns—and I reach for the music again, and think, <u>Good solid floor!</u>

Both of us—skewered John Starfire and I—appear about three feet off the ground near Whirr.

And crash into that floor.

Ow.

Had to be Imperial standard grav, aiya.

Also, why didn't I think *good solid floor* when he was trying to kill me?

John Starfire screams in pain, and coughs blood.

"So you en't dead. Well, what kind of asshole are you?" I say, as if that's somehow a good question to ask this bastard when he's lying here bleeding out. "You flew into the Dark Zone and offered the devil whole planets full of people!"

He twists around and looks at me, tries to say something. Just blood comes out, runs down his handsome chin.

He en't going to answer me. By the look of things, he's on his way out—I stuck that big old sword right through his chest, and must have gotten a lung or an artery or something important. He's got minutes.

He hacks up blood, adding to the puddle he lies in, but then he tries to rise on his hands.

I ought to just stand here and watch him die. That'd be mighty satisfying.

But no, he owes folk too much. I gotta do this aboveboard.

"I en't the right one to ask about justice," I say. "In the spaceways, folk give you trouble, they find themselves out the airlock. But I figure you ought not to die. Ought to stand before the galaxy and admit the Chosen One business was never true."

He tries getting up on his hands, tries speaking, but just coughs up more blood.

I'd better get this scab into a vat, soonwise, if I want him to live. You there?

The music comes rushing back.

Can you get us to a vat? I picture what I'm thinking. Somewhere I can find again, quick. A nice one, though, that'll work quick enough to fill the holes in this fella.

The music goes into a loop, almost like it's thinking.

Whirr is still standing there. "I noticed you both have severe lacerations."

"Oh, you think?" I say.

"Medical automatons have been summoned to deal with your injuries."

"I like you, Whirr," I say.

We hit the node before Whirr can do a thing. Time itself seems to wrap around me, and I almost think I can see all of this moon, and all of Earth below. This moon was what all humans, which was, it seems, my ancestors, looked up and saw when they crawled from the muck. The Earth that was lost, and now is waiting for folk to discover it again.

I look around the next minute, and I'm in a real fancy private shuttle. And there in front of me, a real fancy private vat. Real high-headed fancy stuff. Shining with the best nutrients and skin-builders in the goop. Not just going to patch you up with metal and plastic, but will really put the meat and guts back together.

I grab John Starfire under his bloody shoulders, and drag the big lug over. "Got to do this all aboveboard," I mutter. "Would love to just toss you out an airlock, but that'd just be too easy."

He's a big fella. Hard to get into the vat, even when I get it to open, and the smell of that weird jelly wafts through the shuttle. I get under his shoulder and more of his blood and guts spills all over me, and I toss him in.

He falls into the jelly, and looks at me, and manages to crank out one word. "St—ssss—starfire."

"That's your name, yep."

Only after I get him in there do I realize that the thing

made of music has brought me right back to the monster's den; this has got to be John Starfire's own private shuttle. One look outside confirms it. Night is falling, a completely starless night.

I'm back in the temple on the planet in the Dark Zone. In my own galaxy.

John Starfire's shuttle is parked on the beach just a short walk from the temple.

First I find the aid-packs left in his shuttle and slap some synthskin gel on the leg and breast he cut. That one has bled good, so I find a water-pack and drink the whole thing and I show great personal strength because I resist the urge to look for food.

I go duck into the ocean water real quick, gasping at the cold, to wash his blood and guts off of me. It stings like hell in my breast, but it's nice to be clean.

And then, my sword blazing with blue fire, like a hero in a story, 'cept for being soaking wet and starving, I walk back into the temple. The sense-field is open for me and everything. Scurv is naught to be found—I reckon vi just went back to our shuttle and took a nap.

Just like a hero in a story, I walk on into the temple, and back onto the bridge spanning the abyss, and raise my sword.

And then I ruin the fancy bits of it and say, "Uh, salutes."

The uncorrupted Shir finds me in a rush of music, pours that music over me, swirling notes and riffs and so much music that I feel like it'll lift me up and turn me into a piece of music myself.

It's a bit much, really. "One of these days, slab, I'm going to play you some slick-down. All you need is a beat and a bass. None of this fancy stuff. Get your extradimensional ass moving."

Music wells up. <u>We can join now. We can—</u> I don't know how to represent this *joining* thing it talks about, except to explain the music. The thing sings to me in two different parts, that complement each other and also seem to bounce off each other, and then to represent the joining, they merge. Not joining. *Becoming.*

"Easy now. We joining together—well, I en't picky anyway. But en't you got a name at least?"

It "laughs" at the idea of a name.

"I'll call you Kid. You're a young'un still, as your folk reckon time?"

The music is confused. It has no idea what time is. "Never you mind."

I *feel* this thing more than ever. I reckon I can almost see, and taste, and touch, them musical notes, as strange as that sounds. I could almost reckon I have more senses, feelings I en't got words for, and it's touching all them feelings too.

"This joining," I say to Kid. "It going to change me?"

All is change, says the music, or something along them lines.

"John Starfire thinks—he thinks he can make more of you. More uncorrupted Shir. Long as he lets the spiders have their babies."

The music swoops around me, swirls, waiting.

"He reckons them devils leave this planet alone because they sense you, think of you as one of their own young. And he reckons that if they have more young, and he reaches to them young ones through you, he'll be able to . . ." I don't know the right way to say this. "To pull them in pure space? He'll have a whole bunch of uncorrupted Shir, making a billion new nodes to anywhere in the galaxy, joining with his soldiers, and they'll all be like the Jorians in the stories." This is what he got from studying lots of them memory-crypts, all them piecemeal bits of information from the end of the First Empire. "Is it true? If the Shir reproduce, can we make more like you?"

The corrupted ones cannot be . . . uncorrupted, Kid says through music. Children or parents. They know only hunger now. You can only destroy them.

Aw hell, I was afraid of that. Not that I usually want John Starfire to have the right idea, but this time I really hoped his mad plan had something to it.

<u>They remember just enough to leave me alone, but they do not understand. Their hunger consumes them.</u>

"How'm I supposed to destroy them?"

<u>I do not know.</u>

Kid doesn't know. Hell. I figured that at least with this thing, opening new nodes, we could at least surprise the Shir. But I know the Resistance en't got all the Imperial factories running full-tilt yet. And even if I ran around opening lots of new nodes under every Shir's nose, and tossed a planet-cracker at every single one, they wouldn't be stopped.

"Well, how we going to make more of you?"

<u>I will bear young, because you will bear young.</u>

"Uh, I wouldn't be so sure about that one, I reckon . . ."

<u>You will bear young.</u>

The way the music comes across, there en't nothing iffy about that *will*. "Hang on, Kid. You telling me I'm laden?"

<u>You will bear your child. In time, more and more young will come through your line, and new nodes will open for each of them.</u>

"I'm *laden*? I just fought a battle at the end of space and I just took out the Chosen Oogie and we gonna fight the devil and I'm *laden*?" I didn't realize I fell to my knees till I realize I'm staring down the abyss under this bridge. "I'm going to have a child?"

<u>I shall also mature and bear a child, to match with yours.</u>

"How'm I laden?" I say stupidly, and immediately wonder why the music doesn't smack me up the head. Out the airlock with you, Jaqi. I know *how*. I remember every nice little minute of it. I just . . . do I feel like I been smacked.

"Didn't remember to take that old pill," I say, and it sounds so funny I break out laughing. "That pill! Bill told me, and weren't his face red when he said it, if you get the slack from someone has the right bits, you take the pill or we'll need that much more water and air." And of course Araskar had the right bits, being another cross.

Well, that makes me chuckle. En't two sentients in the whole galaxy less qualified to bear young than myself and Araskar.

<u>You do not want the child?</u>

I manage to get up. "I'm a mess of feelings right now, and I'm talking to a thing what's made of music about whether the devil's gonna eat us all, so now don't seem like an ideal time to go bringing a child into the galaxy."

Kid's music swells around me, and I almost lose track of where I am. I don't know how to say what the music's telling me.

It just feels like hope.

"Hope," I say, and laugh. "I weren't made to hope. I was made to run."

And there's the music, reaching through me, touching all my senses plus a good hundred other feelings. Nothing I can put name to. I see the nodes, all of them, everything the Empire made, stretching through this galaxy and beyond, see a whole universe that can be in our hands.

<u>To exist is to hope.</u>

I remember Bill's, just about ten years ago. The place stinks, but I don't notice, because I'm sniffling, snorting my nose into some tissues. I'm curled up in bed, Bill's arm around me, and the pillow under my head is wet and stinks of my tears.

I'm crying because we've messaged every scab everywhere, and my parents is just gone, just went to do a salvage job and didn't come back, and I en't got a clue where they may be, but all odds on dead. Even Bill's said so. He holds me, and strokes my cornrowed hair and whispers, "Shouldn't be true, bug. Shouldn't ever be true. But 'tis."

I hate him for it, but I know he's right. The galaxy's got a lot of scabs. No one'll miss my parents 'cept me.

I en't let myself think on it in years, but I think I saw that girl in Kalia and Toq. I think I saw them alone and crying and missing their own mater and pater.

Right now, I got the whole universe at my fingers. Which means I can bear a little girl whose mama will always come when she calls.

I stand up and I reckon I feel a little different. "Did we—we join together? Like you said?"

<u>We have become one,</u> Kid says. I reach out, and yep, I can see the nodes in a way I en't never been able to before—like gleams of light in a web that stretches over the whole universe. I can go wherever I want, just by figuring on it. Unlike before, when I had to be close to a node to ken it, now I can just find the node in my head.

I could go anywhere in the universe.

I'll go find Scurv, and we'll get off this planet, and figure out what we're going to do about the devils.

And hell, en't no one like a laden woman for getting spoiled on food. I'm going to invoke the Chosen One's privileges and eat like a black hole.

16

Araskar

SECONDBLADE KINEROTH HAS NOT stopped looking at me funny since he packed me into a shuttle and we hit orbit. We dock and debark with a heavy guard on a Resistance dreadnought. Aranella goes somewhere else on the same ship, as a prisoner, although it sounds like they gave her a good suite.

They take me to a meeting room. I look at the holoscreen where, in a moment, we will get the answer to Aranella's message. The old sigil of the Second Empire, Fifth Navy Division hangs just above the viewscreen. I wonder how long I can fake this.

"I don't trust you for a second," Secondblade Kineroth says. It's just me and him. "Word is that you killed a black ops agent, not that you are one."

"I killed someone who had been compromised," I say. "She was going to betray the Regent. She had adopted, ah, the faith of the Saints."

He looks half-convinced. I'm impressed with myself.

Forty Zarra after a banquet couldn't produce this much shit.

"The way I heard it, your mission was to kill two children, and retrieve the memory-crypt they had stolen. Instead, you turned."

"It was something like that," I say, trying not to let on how fast my mind is racing.

"I'm sure it was, you mealy-mouthed traitor."

"Wait, I'm still slurring?" I move my tongue around. "She fixed my tongue. I don't slur anymore."

"You still mumble," he says like it's a character flaw.

This preoccupies me—I still sound mealy-mouthed? I'm slurring out of habit?—until the door opens and a cross with Joskiya's face enters, bearing the emblem of the Firstblade. "The Regent's wife is secured," she says, and puts a hand to her head. "What's this about our number one target being black ops?"

I wave. "Salutes."

"I'm Firstblade Vanaliel, and you're the traitor." She draws her soulsword. "Talk. I know Black Martha. Who's your handler?"

"Never got a name," I lie. Truth is, Rashiya reported right back to Daddy. A good lie is never too far from the truth, just close enough to be plausible. "You're right—I was supposed to kill those children and take the memory crypt. But there was a girl with them. Just some spaceways girl, but the Thuzerians had plans to prop her up as a rival Chosen One in a bid for power. Both myself and my fellow, ah, agent of Black Martha"—keep the shit flowing, Araskar, don't pause—"we got counter-instructions, at the last moment, to leave the children alone and gather data on the girl. She was supposed to have unusual abilities."

"Unusual."

"You know, like in the stories. They thought she could bring people back from the dead, find lost Earth again. Things like that. The point was, they were the same stories folk tell about J... about the Regent." Don't slip, Araskar, damn it. You are a faithful black ops agent.

"What happened to the other agent?"

"My fellow agent started to believe. Got compromised. I killed her, took her memories, before she talked." Even now, I can't speak of Rashiya without my voice breaking a little. That's good. It'll look good, knowing that I killed someone I cared about. "Then the Thuzerians orchestrated the raid on Shadow Sun Seven."

"To steal back the bluebloods imprisoned there?"

"Exactly," I say. "A rival Son of Stars, who spares the bluebloods and fits a different religious interpretation—you can see the appeal. They've never pledged to John Starfire. Suddenly, every blueblood supporter who used to believe in John Starfire has a new alternative."

"The Regent's explicit instructions were to fire on the Thuzerians, no matter what," Firstblade Vanaliel says. "And kill you in the process."

I shrug. "It's possible the Regent decided he didn't need me after all."

"Or he wanted us to kill this girl. This rival Son of Stars."

"I don't know where she is anymore," I say. Still sticking close enough to the truth. I do know, but *a planet in the heart of the Dark Zone* is, as Jaqi would say, crazing talk.

They look at me a long time, and I wonder just about how long it would take for me to reveal how utterly I am lying.

"Where's the Regent?"

"None of us know." Vanaliel's hand clenches on her sword in a way that reminds me far too much of John Starfire. "No one's heard from him! And suddenly the Shir have attacked four inhabited systems!"

Four. Aranella said three. This is happening too fast. There aren't enough ships in the galaxy, enough planet-crackers, enough shards, to slow it.

Their silence says that they are thinking the same thing.

"The girl," I say, knowing what Aranella told me. "She went into hiding. I bet the Regent went after her."

"Who is your handler?"

I shrug. "I can give you an encrypted node-relay frequency, but not much else." She nods toward the node-relay, and I enter the code from Rashiya's memory.

Hope it still goes right back to John Starfire.

And I hope he's still not in.

There sure is a lot of hope here, considering I've used all my luck up.

The node-relay buzzes, but there's no connection—however, her eyes go wide, and she spins and stares at me. "This is one of the Emperor's private channels. The only person with access to them would be the Regent himself."

I spread my hands, try to look as if this should be obvious. "I don't know who it went to."

"Your reports went to the Regent himself." She exhales. "So that's where he went. To find this rival girl."

"Yes," I say. John Starfire's disappearance is proving very convenient for me. As long as he didn't actually go after Jaqi.

Shit, *did* he go after Jaqi? Is it possible he knew? Is that where he's vanished to?

She turns back to me, and suddenly, face contorting, she half draws her sword. "If you truly believe in the Regent's cause, then you won't care if you die to corroborate your story."

Oh shit. My memories are worth more than my life—the classic cross's problem. "You might want to tell me what you're going to do about the Shir first," I say. "The Thuzerians still believe that I'm an innocent prisoner. You message them and say you need their help to kill the spiders, and you show them you haven't harmed me. They've got at least two working dreadnoughts. How many do you have? Enough to take on the Shir in four separate systems?"

"There is no way the Thuzerians will help us."

"I have their loyalty. They think I've pledged to their Chosen One, remember?"

"You think that'll mean anything to them? When they see you working with us?"

"You really have another choice?" Now I don't have to fake my anger. "People are dying! Does the Resistance actually want a galaxy to rule? Lots of good it'll do you to be in charge of a giant Dark Zone!"

We're both quiet then, as she stares at me and I stare back.

I force a laugh. "Who else is going to save the universe besides us? We have all the guns."

She still doesn't speak. But Kineroth does. "I've had this job for ten hours, and it's the worst job in the universe."

Vanaliel is quiet.

"I didn't much like being Secondblade either," I say. "Listen, just let me talk to the Thuzerians."

"Then we can take your memories," Firstblade Vanaliel says.

I spent all that time on Shadow Sun Seven, and didn't learn a thing about gambling, so I hope I've got a good bluff going. "Then you can. For the Regent."

She sighs and hits a button. "Let the Thuzerians through."

They've been on hold this whole time? I sit back while the monks' masked faces come through, trying not to show my irritation.

"I did not expect to see your face," Father Rixinius says, his mask heaving with his breath. Can't tell through the masks, but Paxin is in the room with them, and at least she looks shocked.

"I didn't expect to see your, ah, mask," I say.

Vanaliel hits me from behind. "Talk."

"They haven't hurt you?" Father Rixinius says.

"No," I say. I lean forward. "I remain faithful. They have not yet hurt me, but they are curious about our faith. About our new Saint. And our agreement."

I focus my gaze on Paxin, although they're just going to see a holo-projection, not anything meaningful from my gaze.

"We must face the children of giants together," I say,

hoping I'm getting my scriptural references right. I never had much time for the Bible; five years out of the vat and I never even got to finish reading my comic books.

"What do you mean?"

"Ah, the agreement," Paxin says. Oh, thank God for writers. Someone needs to help me with the stream of shit. "Yes. That no matter our enemy, we would join them against the Shir."

"What are you—" Father Rixinius stops.

"You've heard."

"Four star systems now," Paxin says. "On all the rogue channels. They're saying well over a trillion sentients dead. The official channels don't have anything, but they never do."

"Attacks on wild worlds," Father Rixinius says, and in case the implication isn't clear, he says, "The Resistance has always known this was coming! They chose to ignore it. You think they care about the wild worlds?"

For a moment, it's silent and I think he might be right. But then Vanaliel speaks. "We never knew. Of course we didn't! You think we wouldn't protect the wild worlds?"

That's a relief. There's a part of the plan John Starfire only shared with his loved ones. *He* didn't care about the wild worlds, but his people should. "So you'll put aside your conflict with the Resistance and go into battle together."

"What?" Before Paxin can help me bluff, Father Rixinius unleashes on Vanaliel. "Your attack killed three thousand Adepts on the dreadnought *Faithful Sword* and a thousand others between battle shuttles and damage to other ships. You have robbed us of a full generation of the faithful. You violated a truce and agreement to exchange a prisoner. Had you not attacked, we would be able to face the Great Belial at full strength!"

"None of it matters," I say, standing up. "None of it. The Shir will eat the entire galaxy while we sit here arguing!"

He waits a moment, does a Grevan thing that I haven't seen before where he lets out three quick exhalations and sucks at his prominent incisors. "Where is she?"

"I don't know," I say honestly.

"Trust in God," Paxin says. "Trust in God, and fight for sentience itself, and the true Son of Stars will appear."

"Plus, if we don't stop them, there'll be no galaxy left to argue over. I don't read the scriptures, Father, but I'm guessing there are a lot of bits in there about fighting the devil."

"There are." He waits a moment. "How is your heavy artillery?"

Vanaliel answers for me. "That was our only planet-cracker back at Llyrixa. I've requisitioned three more from Keil, but the factories aren't even close to their old capacity. Maybe we'll get two more with the supply. As far as we can tell, the Shir are planting new nests in these systems, which means mothering triads."

Father Rixinius looks down at his screen, no doubt reviewing the Thuzerians' information about the Shir. The Thuzerians have sent plenty of brave young monks to die in the Dark Zone over the years, although for them, it was always a choice, unlike the crosses born to it.

The Shir travel faster than light, but their system works differently than the First Empire's nodes. A mothering triad can generate a faster-than-light envoy, and find a likely planet to host eggs. Once they've implanted their eggs, they have a fixed dark node in whatever solar system they've attacked.

They implant their superdense eggs in planets, and since the eggs are sensitive to radiation before they hatch, they need the protection of a planet with a decent magnetic field—meaning everything that the First Empire found suitable for terraforming way back when.

Everything inhabited.

"Have the larvae hatched?"

"In the Aria system, by all accounts, they should have," Vanaliel says. "In Rocina and Varusses, there hasn't been enough time. If we can launch a three-pronged attack on all three systems, we can kill the eggs in two systems and maybe kill the juveniles in Aria."

"The Masked Faith does not have the resources for a three-system attack that will attract adult Shir," Rixinius says. "You saw our entire strength in the attack."

Vanaliel closes her eyes, sighs. I think she must have been hoping that the Thuzerians were hiding another fleet somewhere. "If we don't attack all three systems, those juveniles will hatch and quickly begin to form mothering triads."

"We only have the resources to attack one system, cross."

"All right," I say. "We'll have to just focus on the Rocina system and hope we can cleanse it before the adults arrive. Maybe by then, with all of Keil running at highest Imperial levels, we can still contain those juveniles in the other systems."

"Give us one Imperial day and we will meet you at the node in Rocina," Rixinius says.

Kineroth speaks up, marking what I've suspected—that the boy is useless. "How do we know you'll keep your word?"

I don't recommend ever hearing a Grevan laugh—it sounds a lot like a human coughing out chunks of lung. Father Rixinius bends double with the gagging laugh. "You ask if the servants of God will keep their word? When you pledged to stop the vats, contain the Shir, and restore freedom to the galaxy, and you have done none of these! Do not insult the servants of God and the Saints! How do we know *you* will keep your word?"

"We need a guarantee," Paxin says.

"What do you mean?" Vanaliel says. "Why would we turn on you in battle with the Shir to fight?"

"You've already turned on us in the middle of a peaceful prisoner exchange. And according to our scans of the battle, you weren't even unified."

Vanaliel flushes red. She knows John Starfire gave them a bad order, a countercoup against Aranella, and she followed it anyway.

"We will follow your forces into battle," Paxin says, coming forward in the holo-view. "As long as Araskar is your commander."

"What?"

It takes me a minute to realize that I said it, along with the other two crosses in the room.

"We can't trust any of you," Paxin says. "Except him."

"We are not putting this traitor in charge of the Vanguard," Kineroth spits, but Vanaliel holds a hand up. After a long moment, she says, "We agree."

I don't hear most of this, because I am busy wracking my memories of data dumps for information about the Shir, for information about leading not one but an entire fleet of dreadnoughts into battle—oh, God, I've only ever led ground squads and one disastrous Moth attack.

Oh, God! I don't want to be responsible for all these crosses!

That's what drove me to drugs before!

The connection ends before I can say anything. I stare at Vanaliel.

"If you're a black ops agent, you're the best one that ever lived."

I almost tell her I'm not.

She rips off the emblem of the Firstblade and hands it to me. "Acting Firstblade. Welcome back to the Vanguard. You might as well wear it, or they'll think we're not serious. Step out of line and I put the sword through you."

"I can't . . ." I look down at the emblem, much like the sword emblem I wore as Secondblade, but with three stars above the sword. "This is insane!"

"I know." She shoves the patch into my hands. "But I'm only four weeks old, and I'm not gonna lie: I'm in over my head."

I look between her and the patch. "I'm only five years old."

"That's ancient."

17

Jaqi

I LEAVE THE TEMPLE, go through the courtyard, out the main gate toward where our ship is still sitting on the causeway. I'm all ready to find Scurv, and there's Kalia.

"Kalia? What?" I stand there like a moron, staring at her. "Girl, I told you to stay behind!"

In the light of the new rising sun, she looks like she's been through a war. Her clothes are torn and stained with blood, and she's slumped against the ramp of the ship, clutching something to her side.

"What the hell happened?"

"Jaqi!" She stands up. "I've been waiting for you to come out of there for two nights!"

"Two nights?"

"You were just standing in the center of that bridge and you wouldn't answer anything I said. I actually got out a medkit and scanned you and it kept saying there was nothing wrong."

Huh. I'm guessing that bonding with Kid took a lot longer than I reckoned.

"Where's Scurv?" I noticed what Kalia's cradling. Scurv's guns? What's she doing with vir guns? "Girl, what happened to Scurv?" I walk across the space to stand next to her.

"Scurv was hired to kill you," she says. "You and John Starfire both."

"What?"

"Yeah, vi spoke like you were both being lured here to . . ." Kalia frowns at me. "Was John Starfire in there?"

I don't answer that, because my head is spinning something evil. Scurv was in on it too. "Where's Scurv? Vi got away?"

"Vi's dead," Kalia says. She holds up the guns. "I didn't—I didn't want to, Jaqi, but vi would have killed me."

"Hush." I hold her, but there's no tears from Kalia. Maybe she's just seen too much to have tears to shed. She leans into my chest and I smell something I recognize from Scurv—a weird smell, like a shard-blaster but richer, like it's been mixed with decomposing matter like what was on Swiney Niney. Strange smell.

"You killed Scurv Silvershot? The sheriff of the wild worlds?"

"I had to fight back, Jaqi," she says. "I'm sorry."

"En't a thing to be sorry about, if vi threatened you. Just . . . didn't know you had it in you, girl." I stop, and think about something. "What's left to eat? What you been surviving on?"

"Protein packs from the ship. They're all gone. I'm sorry."

"You . . ." I try not to sound upset. I'm hungry as hell! "You ate all the food?"

"I'm sorry, Jaqi. It's been two days!"

Aw hell. I wasn't really worked up about eating more protein, but damn am I hungry.

"John Starfire came after me," I say. "Scurv must have tattled."

"Vi said that vi was hired to kill both of you. John Starfire's wife did it. No more Chosen Ones, vi said."

That's one way to do it, I suppose. Get rid of any and all special folk. Would have probably taken that tactic myself, were I not prejudiced in favor of keeping my own self alive. "Then I'm guessing Scurv tattled to Aranella back at the Thuzerians' planet, and she gave this location to John Starfire to try and distract him."

"Did you kill him?" Kalia asks.

"You won't believe this one," I say, and I tell her what happened, bouncing back and forth between the node to Earth, and the thing what is made of music, and what happened in the temple, except for the bit where I've been laden, because she don't need to know what Araskar and I were doing afore this mission.

"I reckon I must have fulfilled a whole host of prophecies back there, aiya? Everything in that Bible, checked right off." I figure she's all ready to talk about prophecy, but instead her face looks like she's been gut-shot.

"Jaqi, you're saying John Starfire is still alive?"

"Aiya, yes. He ought to go before the galaxy and tell them how evil he done them."

"Jaqi, that's not how it works!" Kalia stands up. "Where's his ship? There are still lots of crosses that believe in him! You should have let him die!"

"Easy, Kalia," I say. "You killed one troublemaker, you en't got to get bloodthirsty."

"That's not what this is about, Jaqi! You said you were going to kill him. He's too dangerous alive." She looks up at the temple. "His ship's over there?"

"Yep, just on the other side of the temple. He's sitting in a vat. I stuck a big hole in his chest; he en't going nowhere, Kalia."

"It's been *two days,* Jaqi! Come on!"

She don't say much as we run down the beach. It's dark as hell without any stars or a moon above, but she holds up Scurv's guns, letting a shard glow green to illuminate our way.

I'm so hungry it's actually hard to move. Maybe I'll

find food on Starfire's ship.

A thing occurs to me.

Something the music told me about the devils. I keep turning it around in my head, over and over. They don't feel a thing but hunger.

Easy to think on now.

I know something about hunger, and I know that it's real tough to think when you got a hole right through your belly. Can't think on a thing except how much you want a piece of nice fresh food, whether it be a bit of meat or, Starfire bless me, a fresh cold ripe tomato.

But you feel other things. You just have a bit of trouble taking other things seriously, what with that hunger. Them devils have got to feel a few other things, but it's hard to really deal with it over the hunger.

"Jaqi!" Kalia says. "Jaqi, you said his ship was a short walk from the temple?"

"Aiya, not much of a walk at all. Why?"

She waves her hand at the empty shore in front of us. "Shouldn't we have reached it by now?"

I keep going, not answering Kalia. Hoping I don't have to answer this.

But sure enough, we come up on a place where the ground has been churned up fierce, just like a ship took off here. Bits of bulbous glass, superheated, are scattered with the sand.

Kalia doesn't say a word. I just look up, like I'm going to catch the ship in the sky. But no, I can feel it. The node in orbit's been opened and passed through already.

"Jaqi," I say, and slap a hand over my face. I reckon the Bible says plenty about how a Chosen Oogie en't supposed to let the Usurper go.

18

Araskar

TURNS OUT THAT KEIL was running at top capacity, so the Resistance manages to drum up eight dreadnoughts, matching the two the Thuzerians bring.

Ten dreadnoughts emerge into the Rocina system, to face the Shir.

Rocina was a nice blue world once, no doubt. I've been reading about it, briefing myself, as one apparently does before leading a naval mission.

The planet is—was—an independent federation of city-states built on large islands. No landmass big enough to be called a continent. Good vacation spot. Lots of places to swim, to hike, to boat, supportive to human life and a variety of other sentient life, including at least one semiaquatic race that had been there long enough to forget whether or not they ever crossed. No interest in the Empire—they could offer better drugs and delights illegal in the Empire by staying independent.

It's not nice now.

Space is big, and so the node is still far enough from the planet that we have to see it all magnified on sensors. And what we see of Rocina is a broiling black marble. Red and white lightning flashes through the black clouds marring the surface. A thick black thread, big enough to dwarf our entire fleet, emerges from the planet and vanishes into space. It twists and spins like a huge cyclone, pulling in the light.

A Shir node; a wormhole no one but the big spiders can use.

"Any refugees?" I ask. "Any ships we need to get out of the way?"

"Scanning. There's plenty of debris, Firstblade."

"*Acting* Firstblade." I can't help it; I look over at Vanaliel.

"Plenty of debris. Lots of ships damaged in the escape from the planet. Sweeping for life-signs and finding very little."

"Is *very little* nothing?"

She pauses. "No, Firstblade. Some evidence of sentients on a ship adrift in the orbit of Rocina's main planet. Probably refugees from the attack."

"Send a drop ship and a Moth escort." I try to sound like a man who deserves his command. "And once they've made contact, launch the planet-crackers."

"We don't have that luxury," Kineroth says.

Vanaliel doesn't speak. She's wearing no rank emblem, but she's standing to my left, and she eyes me.

"My order stands, Secondblade," I say. I motion for him and Vanaliel to follow me into the communications chamber just off the bridge.

"Don't counteract me on the bridge," I say to Kineroth as soon as the door to the comm room closes. Once again, an old Fifth Navy symbol stares back at me. "This is hard enough already."

"A handful of sentients aren't worth a delay that could get us killed, Acting Firstblade," Kineroth says.

"No scans are showing the mothering triad, are they?" I say. "We're still unnoticed."

"No scans have shown the mothering triad," Vanaliel interjects. "But they have ways of hiding from us. I think you forget that for fighting Shir, this crew is still green."

"I haven't forgotten," I snap. "We're all green. I've never been to the Dark Zone." I pause and add, "But it is what we were designed for, you know."

Vanaliel and Kineroth both look away. No one's used to this. It's a lot to ask of a cross who's swallowed John Starfire's propaganda whole, about how we were meant for more than to die in the Dark Zone, how we're sentient and we can have our own art, our own worlds, our own children and grandchildren. Now we're facing the fate we all rejected. We all believed what John Starfire said when he made peace, even though that was too good to be true.

Father Rixinius and the Thuzerians pop up on the holo-table, with none of the distortion that usually marks the node-relay. "You will launch the planet-cracker?"

"We have a rescue mission going in first," I say. "The minute they verify whether there are sentients alive in that debris field, we launch the planet-crackers. Two planet-crackers for the planet—hopefully the first will hit its target and we can reroute the second one to deal with any adult Shir in-system."

"I hope you're right," Father Rixinius says, and tunes out.

"Leave me," I say to the Firstblade and Secondblade.

I stay in the room and close my eyes. Jaqi, I wish you could hear me.

If I had her here, I still wouldn't be able to say everything—to say how insane this feels, to say how I've dodged about five kinds of death, and every time I thought of her.

Instead, I make a private call within the ship. If anyone notices, they'll be too distracted to comment on it.

Aranella's holo-figure comes up on the table. "What is it?"

I swallow. I can't read a face through a holo, and I can't help wondering what she's thinking. Is she thinking about how I lied about Rashiya's memories? Is she thinking about my request for forgiveness?

"I've got command," I say. "We're moving against the Shir. Do you have any idea where, uh, the Regent, is?"

She sighs. "He just disappeared. He could be dead. He could have gone into the Dark Zone again. Or he could show up any minute now. I can't predict what he'll do."

"I hope he stays quiet," I say.

"Tell me something, Araskar," she says, and I can hear how much it hurts her to say my name, even.

"What is it?"

"Were you serious about forgiveness?"

"Yes."

"Promise me I'll go free. If you have any power over the situation, promise me I'll live. I want to go back to my surviving children."

I don't say anything. This acting Firstblade thing will last exactly as long as my bullshitting lasts. I don't know that I can promise that.

"I'll forgive you, if you promise me I can see my children again." She leans forward. "I'll forgive you for lying to me."

I slowly nod. "I promise."

"Good."

I don't say much, just turn off the holo, and sit for a moment. I don't feel any different, and yet somehow it feels like something has changed.

Forgiveness. Hope.

I damn myself for thinking that life sounds so good.

And then, I get up and go back to the bridge. Nothing to do but wait some more, and watch Rocina burn. The sensors indicate that the Shir eggs have not yet begun to pupate. They are just incubating for the time being, growing a few thousand nightmares. Once they hatch, they'll need to take on material for their inner furnaces. I call up all the charts and pictures from my data dump. They'll stretch out and flatten until they can absorb a sun or a gas giant big enough to compact into a nuclear reaction, to power their guts.

Only those big planet-cracking shards will take out the Shir eggs. Imperial campaigns have all been meant to contain the Dark Zone, killing as many spore-producing adult Shir as possible. Since they never seem to die naturally, and the adults have the opposite reaction as their larvae to space's background radiation—they thrive off it—it's a difficult prospect. Shards kill Shir, though, and although it takes several planet-crackers to kill an adult Shir, or so my data dump tells me, it will only take one to break a planet that's hosting their eggs.

It feels like a year, but it's only twenty minutes before the rescue ships confirm. "We have life signs for the rescue mission. And atmos inside the ships. Beginning rescue mission."

Kineroth mumbles something about being too late. I ignore it.

"I want planet-cracker launch." I indicate both dreadnoughts that have intercepted and carried the new planet-crackers. "Two squads of Moths each for protection, one from *Thalator,* one from *Kassarath.*" We like old-timey Jorian names for the dreadnoughts too. "*Thalator* will move to the far side of the planet with the Thuzerians. Set up orbit."

"It will take an hour for the planet-crackers to fall," Vanaliel says.

"An hour is a short time for monsters the size of a star," I say. "Maybe they won't notice."

I continue to take reports, to wait, so on edge that my teeth practically chatter.

The planet-crackers are making a good pace, and we keep the second far enough back that we can save it if the first one lands normally, and the mission matters. The rescue mission reports back—they have landed on a transport ship, and evacuated a few hundred sentients who just escaped Rocina in time.

The sentients are sick, distraught. But alive.

All things considered, my mission might be working.

"Adjusting the first planet-cracker's velocity to fall in with the orbit," the communications officer says. "We're nearing the point of no return. As soon as we can plot a steep descent into the orbit, Rocina is as good as cracked."

"Crack those eggs," I say, and let a little smile come to my face.

"Wait."

I turn and look at the comm officer. "What do you mean, wait? Is it . . ."

"It's not the Shir. A ship has just appeared in system, and it's transmitting on . . . it's transmitting on a frequency that clears all our codes. Even classified ones."

"What?"

"There's visual and audio both. Should I put it on-screen?"

I have a sinking feeling I know who it is. I look behind me, and before I can say anything, Kineroth says, "On-screen."

The comm officer obeys.

And John Starfire fills our viewscreen.

"My Resistance," he says, his voice barely above a whisper. He's pale, sweating, his face marred with blood and some green gunk that looks like it might have come out of a vat. He's been hurt, and hasn't taken the time to heal properly.

"Regent!" Vanaliel stands next to me. "Patch us in to the Regent!"

"I'm trying, sir," the comm officer says. "He's not receiving."

"My Resistance," he says. "I have returned. I am sorry for what I must order you to do. You must trust me. The Shir's young must be allowed to hatch. I repeat. They must be allowed to hatch."

Kineroth raises a hand. "Reroute the planet-cracker."

"Wait," I say. "No. You can't stop it. It's just about to fall."

"He's switched to receiving, sir. We're patched in to the Regent," the comm officer says.

And John Starfire looks up from the viewscreen at me, and his eyes burn. "You? *You?* Traitor!"

I look over at Vanaliel, whose eyes are fire.

I draw my sword. "There is no way I'm allowing a planet full of Shir eggs to hatch. No matter what the Regent orders."

Everyone on the bridge looks between each other, back at me, back at each other.

Then Vanaliel lunges for me, a blow meant to run me through.

And I'm weak and wounded still, and though I get my own blade up and deflect hers, it's not perfect. She slashes a chunk from my nice new leg. I go down on one knee.

"It's crazy," I yell, as I block another of her blows. I draw my short sword and slash at her leg. She dances back. Despite the pain, I get up on my leg, leaking blood and synthskin.

"Listen to me now," John Starfire says. "Do not listen to the traitors, who have tried to prop up their own false prophet. I have been to the very end of the universe, my Resistance. I have seen Earth that was lost. And the new generation of Shir is not what you think. They can be turned. They can be changed."

Vanaliel comes at me with a standard thrust, typical out-the-vat stuff. I turn it with my short sword and tag her arm with my long blade. She twists, too fast, her own short sword an inch from my belly when I stop it.

We stand there, hilts locked.

"You were always a traitor," Vanaliel says. "You're as bad as the Regent's wife. Or worse."

"Listen to him! He's telling you not to kill the Shir! He's siding with the devil itself! That is betrayal!"

"Planet-cracker adjusting velocity," the comm officer says. "We will change to a stationary orbit until orders say otherwise."

"Good," Kineroth says.

Vanaliel shoves, with all her strength. My leg gives out and I crash against the wall. The cold steel of her sword touches into my neck, and then she draws back for the killing blow—and waits, short sword at my throat, long sword drawn back for a stab. "I want to leave your memories for the Regent, but my hand just might slip, traitor."

"Oh yeah," I say, struggling to get up, until she kicks me in the belly again. I cough out the words, the steel biting into my throat with each word. "The one working with the Shir's not the traitor. I see."

Doubt mars the rage in Vanaliel's face.

"You will see." John Starfire's voice reaches a feverish, tinny pitch. "You will see. Let them hatch, and they will come to me, and I will change them. Can you feel the truth in these words?"

"Something's changed in the planet, uh, Secondblade," the comm officer says. "I think the pupation process is beginning."

Voices fill the comm. There's Father Rixinius protesting on the comm. "Do not stop the planet-cracker's course! Do not let the juveniles hatch! In the name of God and the Saints—"

And then a voice that makes my mouth dry, my skin shiver, makes me feel like I'm frozen in the grip of the pinks again. A voice that kills all my friends before me once again. A voice that makes Rashiya's dead eyes look back at me.

<u>We hear you, little things.</u>

A scream.

The ship makes a sound like a can opening.

Everything lurches—and suddenly we're without

gravity, the air is cold, and all I see is a faint, sickly blue light on the sensors—

And then the emergency power takes hold, and I am looking through a sense-field. On the other side of the sense-field, half the bridge spins away in vacuum, against faint blue-white lines that fill space, like a web cast over the darkness.

Gravity slams me to the floor, the generators going to twice the power to keep us rooted—and then the gravity generators fail and I fly up again in zero.

Kineroth floats off into vacuum, dead and still glaring at me. The poor comm officer still clings to her comm, on the wrong side of the atmos.

In front of me, Vanaliel floats, shedding globules of blood where the sense-field took off both her legs. But at least most of her is on the oxygenated side.

And I'm not dead yet. All of two feet from open space.

I leap to catch her, kick off against the sense-field despite the shock that runs through me, and pull her body back toward the lift.

And through the sense-field, out in space, a dark sun rises in front of Rocina's star, and I detect in the dim blue light a thousand legs, a thousand eyes, teeth like planet-sized spars.

<u>We told you, little one, little John.</u> Their voices hit me like the sight of my friends' dead bodies, like the with-

drawals from the pinks. <u>You are not the one.</u>

Sickly blue filaments spin through space, hit the protective sense-field and the ship screams again. The Shir are attacking us.

I fly through zero into the lift, slam the door closed, and it plunges through the ship toward the hangar. Blood rushes in globules from Vanaliel's severed legs, spatters all over me.

<u>You are not the one.</u>

I think I hear John Starfire scream.

I'm guessing the Shir just broke that truce.

19

Araskar

THE LIFT TUMBLES AND screams to a halt. I wrench the doors open. The corridor is awash in pale yellow emergency lights. Debris tumbles through the air in zero—bits of a bulkhead, an empty shard-blaster.

I need to get to a comm. And a med-bay. Vanaliel's severed arteries are spraying the blood rapidly, little bubbles spinning through the air and splattering against the wall, rebounding onto me.

"Araskar," she gags. "Araskar. I didn't—"

"It's okay, soldier, I forgive you your insubordination." There's got to still be a functioning med-bay. And then—what then? I need a comm. I need to tell Rixinius we're still fighting.

I scramble through the hall, dodging the debris, much of which is coming quickly enough to kill. The zero makes it much easier to move; I just have to be careful not to get going too fast and smear myself against the bulkhead.

Vanaliel chokes on her blood, tries to speak but gags on the words.

We should be on the same floor as the node-relay. I'm going to have to call for help to everyone. Necros. Kurguls. Suits—anything with a gun.

Not that anyone in the galaxy has anywhere near the military might the Navy has. Had.

"You know," I find myself saying aloud, "if I could go back in time to the invasion of Irithessa, I would have to point out that peace with the Shir was wishful thinking." If only I had woken up then. I was way too interested in finishing the mission so I could get my hands on some drugs.

We're halfway down the hall, and I dodge a wrench flying through the air so fast it could take my head off. I realize Vanaliel is talking. "Araskar," she mutters. "I wanted to—I wanted to be a musician. I wanted to play—"

"Plenty of time for what you want to be," I say.

"I wanted to live," she says.

"You'll live!"

There's emergency vats on every level, the kind of place you can stick a wounded soldier for containment if there's a hull breach. I pull the wires that open the wall and put Vanaliel inside. She stares up at me as the green goo of the vat closes over her legs.

Kid was fresh out of the vat. Three weeks ago everything she knew was contained in one data dump. Today she's another near-dead cross, in a ship full of the same.

"Just hang on, all right?" I say. "Automatic recall will take over without the bridge. The ship will fire on automatic until it runs out of shards, and then it'll go back to the node. You'll live."

As long as the automatic recall isn't damaged. Considering that the gravity's gone, I'm guessing the recall is.

She looks so scared.

I have to leave her there.

I reach a node-relay station and turn it on. It screeches like it's an animal in pain.

"Rixinius, tell me you hear me!"

It takes a long time before a much-battered voice comes on. "Araskar? You live?"

"I live. Tell me the situation."

"Two full mothering triads. Six Shir. They've destroyed two of our ships already, and one of the planet-crackers—the second one, the one that was still on course for the planet."

"Where's the first one? Still in orbit around Rocina?"

"Still in orbit. It's too close for them to risk triggering it. The juveniles are hatching, Araskar. If you can reach the planet-cracker, disrupt its orbit so it falls to the planet, you can at least kill the eggs."

"My ship is in no shape to do that."

"Araskar, in the name of God and all Saints, you must drop that planet-cracker. We will stand against the darkness now—but you *must*. By any means."

The entire ship rocks, and the comm goes dead.

Shit in space.

Well, there will still be Moths in the hangar bay. And a Moth will get me to that planet-cracker faster than any shuttle. It'll be nice and comfortable in there, my body cushioned by the Moth's inner goo against the g-forces of spaceflight.

Just one other thing to do.

I run back down the hallway, dodging more debris, bouncing off the bulkheads. At one point the gravity generator flickers, and I am unexpectedly slammed to the ground, but the adrenaline is still working, because I get up, and a second later we're back to zero. I'm leaving my own globules of blood from where Vanaliel cut my leg, and it hurts like hell and I probably shouldn't be running on it, but at least the zero makes it a little easier to swim along.

I reach Aranella's room.

Thankfully, the doors don't protest when I force them. Even secure locks will be disabled under emergency power.

Aranella springs out of the darkness with a blazing soulsword—and stops.

She stares at me. Both of us lock eyes, stare across the darkness.

"You going to kill me?" I ask.

A long moment between us, between her eyes, blazing with rage, between her sword and my hand on my own hilt.

She sheaths the sword. "No."

We make it to the lift, but it's not where I left it—but in zero, we just spring down the shaft. About halfway down the whole ship shakes, and we're thrown against the side of the shaft. Gravity, but the wrong way.

"We're under thrust," Aranella says, from where she's pressed against the side of the lift. "Emergency retrieval, heavy burn under unthunium thrusters. Moving back toward the node."

"It was your husband that did this. You were right. He wants the Shir to reproduce."

"I heard him," she says. "I patched into the main channels."

"Why they hell does he want this?" I say.

"He spent a lot of time with the scriptures," Aranella says. "You tend to see what you want in the Bible after a while. He wanted peace with the Shir, so he found a section that said so."

Under thrust, pressed against the side of the lift, we climb down, hand over hand, the side of the lift becoming the floor—until the ship shifts again, and we start to fall. I cling to the handholds, try to ignore the pain in a leg I'm suddenly putting weight on.

"The hangar," she says, and drops down to the next level. "Come on!"

I drop down next to her, and crumple. "Ah, shit, my leg!"

She pulls me to my feet. "You can whine about your leg later."

We enter the hangar bay.

There are still plenty of Moths, curled up in their pods along the walls. The ship shakes again, and we're fighting all sorts of g-forces as it goes under emergency thrust. Luckily there are handholds here for emergency zero. I limp along the ground, pulling myself via the railing holds as gravity shifts on me. Come on, leg. One step, one more step, and then the Moth.

"It would be so easy not to remember," Aranella says, from where she's similarly crawling along next to me.

"What?" I say, through a haze of pain.

"All the pain would be gone if the memory was. Sometimes I feel like all I have are memories of hope."

"Memory's blade cuts deepest of all," I say.

"Didn't take you for a philosopher," she says.

"I'm well read. Had the entire collection of Scurv Silvershot comic books."

I reach the Moth.

It only takes a few seconds to open the pod with the override code, and the Moth tumbles from the pod and expands. Its wings, meant for light atmos, won't do anything out there in the vacuum, but here they seem necessary, weirdly beautiful, the microfilaments gleaming in the emergency lights.

"Not dead yet," I mutter as I climb into the Moth. I drive my soulsword into its fin-brain, and I "see" through the Moth's segmented eyes, giving me a much broader field of perception and a stranger sense of depth all around me.

The Moths rise, each ridge along the wing humming together, each a tiny blade, like part of a helicopter. They help us to hover in the hangar bay's atmos, and launch us despite the ship's thrust through the small hole in the wall, right through the sense-field.

We soar out of the hangar bay, into the darkness.

Vacuum brings a weirdly peaceful silence. Oh, sure, debris is everywhere, and the Moth corrects course a good sixty times in the first minute of the flight to avoid debris flying at high speed. Most of the debris is made up of pieces of the ship I was just on. Some of the debris is made up of cross bodies, flying so fast they could smash through anything without a decent sense-field.

In the distance, dark shapes of Shir move back and

forth through the system, spinning those sickly colored blue webs at the tiny lights darting for them. They've attempted to spin the web around the planet, to protect their juveniles, but the planet-cracker is in a stationary orbit, my sensors tell me, and they can't risk triggering it, changing its orbit.

That shouldn't be too tough. As long as I can hit the planet-cracker hard enough, I can just send it on a descent toward Rocina, and it'll break open the planet before the juveniles all have a chance to hatch.

"Araskar," Aranella says.

"What is it?"

"The refugee rescue."

Ah shit, she's right. There in front of us is a damaged drop ship, trying to limp back to the dreadnought. Carrying all those people I was so careful to rescue.

"Raise the dreadnought *Thalator*."

The Moth's comm array buzzes, and I say, "This is Acting Firstblade Araskar to anyone who's listening. Do not retreat. Do not allow automatic recall. Rescue ship is still attempting to rendezvous with the node. Cover for them before you make a retreat. Understood?"

No answer.

"I think you burned your bridges there," Aranella says.

That's when the Shir notice us.

Half-blue, half-white lines spin through space toward

us, striking for our Moths and the drop ship carrying the refugees. I fire, shards spinning bright red through space, and I manage to cut the Shir's threads, red shards breaking the eerie blue apart.

"You escort them back," I tell Aranella.

"You're going to need help," she says.

"Then come back and help me," I say. "Let me get to the planet-cracker."

I know the easiest way about this mission, as my Moth spins through space, dodging the filaments of Shir energy that reach with their sickly blue fingers for me. The easiest thing to do is get my ship under the planet-cracker, fire on the shard, and let the resultant explosion take out me—and the planet.

But I'm going to try to drop it on the planet. Because . . . "I don't want to die," I mutter as my Moth gets closer. "I want to live. Not what I should want, I know." It's funny, how loud my voice sounds, when it's the only noise inside the Moth, when all of silent space closes around me. "I like the idea of living. Crazing, I know."

It's closer now. The planet-cracker is a single white wedge hanging above the black storm of Rocina. I run over every potential scenario. I need the orbit to degrade quick. As in, I need it just to fall.

The Moths have auxiliary arms, two long things hanging beneath the main pod. They're not going to be that easy to manipulate, but if I can land on the planet-cracker without attracting attention, I can reprogram it just by patching in. If worse comes to worst, I can go under the planet-cracker's shell with the Moth and tear out the guidance system.

I'm afraid both of those options will take too much time.

I set the course, and come closer to the white wedge.

Thank God the Thuzerians are keeping the Shir busy. Blue-white filaments spin through space toward me, but none of them are precise—the Shir spinning them are distracted by the Thuzerians' attack. Through the Moth's vision, I just see the Thuzerians' attack, a barrage of red shards in the darkness near one of the Shir.

Still, there was supposed to be an escort with this, and going by the amount of shattered Moth debris I'm scanning, the Shir got everyone. Killed all my troops.

Don't get overconfident, Araskar. Just do the job.

Closer now. The white wedge of the planet-cracker fills my sensors.

And then my Moth touches down on the planet-cracker. The insectile body settles onto the wide swath of white metal, clinging to the surface through hooks in the auxiliary arms.

"Back here again," I say. Hasn't been long since the last

planet-cracker. "We have to stop meeting like this."

Through my soulsword, I tell the ship to manipulate the Moth's auxiliary arms. The guidance system has been remote-controlled this entire time. A quick access to the control panel tells me it is code-locked.

I can only do basic manipulation here—I have to patch into the planet-cracker's brain to adjust this.

Best option is to climb just far enough underneath to tear out the guidance system, like I did before. Or grip the entire thing with the Moth's arms and fly it into orbit myself.

Just as my Moth crawls toward the nose of the ship, something red flashes by me. And then the Moth's alarms scream, and my ship spins, and nearly goes flying off the planet-cracker.

"Don't do it." John Starfire's voice, on a universal channel.

Do I ignore him, or do I talk back, and make this worse?

He lands his own Moth on the planet-cracker behind me. I spin mine around, dragging my ship's damaged end, and both of us face each other, in our insectile carapaces, across the distance of the ship.

"Come out and face me, Araskar," he snarls. "Traitor."

"You remember what you told me," I say. "That you didn't know if you were the Chosen One, but you had to act like it? Turns out you aren't! I'm sure that's a load off."

"This is all because I trusted you."

"I can hear you pawing your sword, you paranoid old bastard."

He skitters toward me, and rears up, and his Moth's wings, whirring with their hundred tiny blades, buzz toward my own Moth's face. I back off. As strategies go, this isn't a bad one. As long as we're in vacuum we won't need these wings, but because I'm damaged, I can't move like he can.

He backs my Moth up, against the rim of the planet-cracker. "You want to live, Araskar. You took my daughter from me. You took my people from me. And you still want to live."

He's right. I still want to live. It's my weakness now. The universe needs an Araskar who is willing to die here.

I close my eyes. *I'm sorry, Jaqi. I wanted you more than anything. More than drugs. More than freedom. More than Rashiya.*

And I fire.

My shard hits his Moth and knocks it nearly off the planet-cracker, breaking up its wing into a thousand pieces of space debris. I fire again, and blow off the back of his carapace, and then his Moth goes spinning into space, vanishes against the darkness of Rocina.

"Traitor," he shouts through the comm—and then goes silent.

The planet-cracker roars and lurches as shard-fragments pinhole it, breaking through the metal shield. The shard underneath it is destabilized now, red and roaring. It's going to blow up under me.

I grip the planet-cracker with the auxiliary arms and pilot my Moth down, down, down into the gravity well. Alarms scream in my ears, scream that the ship is damaged, that the shard has destabilized and the planet-cracker is losing integrity—

Upper atmos buffets my ship. The Moth compensates by using the wings, but the controls aren't working right—the auxiliary arms are burning now, tearing away—the hundred small fragments of the wings rip away under the pressure of the gravity well and the atmos and burn as the shard destabilizes—lightning streaks across the clouds below me, and the gravity well sucks at me—

I break away, leaving bits of my Moth still clinging to the planet-cracker. I climb, climb, climb toward space.

Gravity and upper-atmos wind tears at my ship, sends it careening, but I lean on the thrusters. Just a little space. Just a little thrust—

The Shir scream in my ears.

Below me, the planet-cracker vanishes into the black clouds of Rocina.

My Moth makes hard vacuum again.

It's instantly cold, the containment breached. Space is full of sickly blue-white filaments, the Shir's webs cast across this entire system. My damaged ship limps along, but John Starfire has damaged the main thrusters. We won't make it beyond orbit.

Below me, Rocina erupts in a massive plume of red.

The darkness rises before me. A thousand eyes like black holes, a planet-sized mouth with jagged spars of teeth. The Shir's roar tears through me, stabs icepicks into every inch of my body, shreds my mind.

<u>You little thing.</u>

But over the roar, I hear music.

20

Jaqi

"ROCINA SYSTEM." Kalia gets off the comm that connected us up to the Thuzerians. "To fight the Great Belial."

"I've been to Rocina," I say, trying to ignore the sick feeling in my gut as I reach out for the node. The devils already made their move, and some Chosen One I am, three steps behind, lost the Usurper, still without a plan.

"I've never even heard of it."

"Nice place, they say. Well, I didn't go no further than the orbital platform, but the planet's supposed to be nice."

"What did you do there?"

"Well, since you're becoming a woman and all, what with the killing people, I can tell you that I got high as five suns. Don't really recall what happened after that. Woke up next to a fluid sentient."

Kalia makes a little noise of disgust. Nice to see we en't changed, aiya? I say spaceways things, she disapproves.

It's the same whether I've bonded with a pure-space thing made of music, and whether she's got Scurv's guns coming out of her sides.

"What do you think we'll see on the other side?" Kalia asks me.

"The devil himself," I say, and I reach out for the node. I try not to show Kalia how scared I am, but my hand shakes on the lever. I been into a lot of scrapes, a lot of dodgy bits, but this en't the fighting pit, this en't the guts of Shadow Sun Seven, this en't even a swordfight against John Starfire. This is the darkness. The spiders. This is them things who haunt my nightmares and the Chosen Oogie *en't got a plan.*

You grow up in the spaceways, you learn a few things. Always, always, always check the seals, the air, and the water. Salvage can save you. Never turn down parts or water. Use the grav generator even if it itches you, otherwise it'll hurt too bad when you go planetside.

And stay the hell away from the Dark Zone.

I'm about to do the dumbest thing any spaceways girl has ever done.

"Wait, Jaqi. Hang on." Kalia looks up at me. "The Thuzerians just raised us again. They say they have a message for you. They want me to put it on audio." Kalia hits the button to put audio on the whole ship, despite the fact that we're running evil low on the batteries.

And it en't no stuffy monk's voice I hear. It's Z. His voice is raspy, and he don't mention honor, which makes me wonder if it's really him for a moment, but I make out what he's saying.

"Jaqi," he gasps, as if he's just run a mighty race. "Jaqi. The Shir sing. They sing."

And then the node-relay cuts off.

"Interference," Kalia says. "Do you think it's John Starfire—"

"No," I say. The devils sing? Them what is monsters, who don't remember nothing but hunger, they sing? I feel like I been given the last bit of a puzzle, only I need time to turn the puzzle to make it fit.

"Z? Why Z?" Kalia asks.

I don't answer. They sing. So I was right about a thing—they don't just feel hunger, it's just that hunger makes it hard to feel anything else.

Hey. I send out a feeling toward that sense of Kid. You there?

The response is a big swelling of music, like some kind of triumphant march. Easy, we en't won yet. Listen, how do them Shir do what they do? How do they travel faster than light without pure space?

The music sends what I already know; they got their own system of nodes, it just en't going through the pure-space dimension what we all know, where the music lives.

Traveling faster than light hurts them, Kid "says." I'm still translating from music here. They will only risk it to try and bear their larvae.

What happens if they try to go back into your pure space, to change back?

The music is clear on one thing—them Shir cannot change back. They used to exist as creatures of pure space, and regular old space twisted them. It's just a thing that happened. But what happens if they try?

I don't know, says Kid.

What happens if they remember what they was? I ask.

That's beyond Kid. No music answers me.

"Jaqi," Kalia says. "The Thuzerians sent a report about the battle. It's . . . it's not going well. There's two full mothering triads there. Araskar's trying to hit the planet and stop the eggs, but they say . . ." Kalia trails off into silence.

Araskar. That big slab better live; he went and got me laden! "Let's go, then," I say.

"Jaqi . . ."

"What do them scriptures say about this?"

"The son of stars faces the children of giants, and he is armed but with faith."

I draw Taltus's old sword. The blue flame sprouts up, a few flickering bits along the length of the black sword. "Faith! There you go."

"It also says, *the children shall be the change, and the change shall be the children.*"

"And there you go." I carefully sheathe the sword—I can do that, at least, without slicing myself up—and point at Scurv's guns, what she wears at her hips now. "You're a child, and look how much you changed."

"Jaqi, what are you going to do against six fully grown Shir?"

"I'm going to try a thing," I say.

"A thing?"

"I en't got fancy words, girl! A thing!"

It's so easy now. Before, I felt the node, and I felt where we needed to go, and it just got us there, but it weren't foolproof—sometimes I messed up and got the wrong node, sometimes I needed the codes, or the Suits to hack it. It was like that instinct, like hunger or slack or one of those things in the back of the brain.

Now, with the music in my head, the whole of the galaxy's nodes spread out for me, like points on a map. "Rocina."

So we go.

Into the music, and spinning out—

"Jaqi!" Kalia says. "Shields!"

Debris is everywhere as we spin out of the node. I already had the sense-field up, but the debris batters it, makes the ship scream. I grab the controls and pilot us through and away—I seen plenty of debris fields, and though I en't no book reader, I can tell what the computer's telling me about the speed of the debris.

Bits of cross bodies, bits of metal and bulkheads and all the stuff from the innards of the Navy ships flies away from our sense-field.

"Uh, Jaqi." Kalia's voice is hoarse, gasping in the cockpit. "Jaqi!"

"What—ah."

Sensors take a minute to recognize what's in front of me. By the time they start telling me I'm well and truly out the airlock, I already know.

The massive, dark forms move in front of us. They're so huge they have their own gravity well, pulling at us, trying to suck us down into their dark maws, their thousand spars of teeth.

I grab the sword, but the whole cockpit goes dark, and the blue flame of the sword goes out, is replaced with a light I recognize, from when I hit the Dark Zone before. Faint light, kind of white, kind of blue in its own way, like the glow of rotting stuff in the forest floor of Swiney Niney.

And I hear them.

<u>We have found you again.</u>

<u>We will not let you go.</u>

<u>We . . .</u>

Faith, Jaqi, faith. Faith. Hell, I can't seem to think. What'd I do back on Shadow Sun Seven? On Trace? I en't no miracle worker, this is madness, this is . . .

<u>We have found you. You who will fill our hunger.</u>

No, I had hope. En't hope without fear.

Behind their voices, that music's still moving. My mother's voice, singing her field-hand song. *Bend, pull. Bend, pull.* That little song still sounds, in the cold of my mind.

The devils speak, and I can almost feel what they feel. Cold, empty hunger, stretching across all of space. A thousand dead star systems, all eaten up, all hunger. So hungry for more, hungry to extinguish stars and implant their eggs in planets. Their memories are pain, and hunger. Their existence is pain, and hunger. There is no room for anything else, with that hunger.

And I can see their web too. It's a faster-than-light web, like the nodes, but it sits right on the surface of pure space, like black cracks in something bright and whole.

They almost remember. Something, stuck in the back of the brainpan, tells them they wasn't always hungry.

I reach out for Kid. "Help me out," I say. "I'm gonna try singing to them."

I ignore Kalia shouting, and I open up to Kid. Same thing I did back on Trace, when I healed Z—I reached out and joined that music of the universe, the swelling, pulsing music that Kid puts out with my mother's simple field song.

Something about music. En't never put much thought to it, but a beat brings out things in you too deep for words. I had these thoughts before. Like it's rain falling into my ears and hitching a ride through my bloodstream, notes meeting each other and merging together down in my guts. Pouring up out through my eyeballs. Like light through a scrap of worn fabric.

Like a note deep in my belly, a whole new note made just for this new life inside me.

And so I let Kid's music flow out, like my mother's simple field song is channeling it. Not only do I let it flow out to the Shir in front of me, but I reach into their dark web, their dark nodes.

I let the music flow through the Dark Zone.

The dark nodes was sitting like black cracks on pure space, and now the cracks vanish. Them dark nodes is still there, but they's just *nodes* now, absorbed into the rest of pure space.

And now the Shir turn.

They hear the music.

<u>It is us.</u>

<u>It is us.</u>

All the Shir across the whole of the Dark Zone hear Kid's music. And they remember what they were.

And as one, they reach out for Kid.

<u>Kid, uh, you okay? They're trying to—</u>

They reach out, and they all jump into the nodes.

For a half second I figure I've ruined everything. The Shir can use pure space itself now, and they're going to go after Kid, and they'll . . .

<u>Jaqi.</u> Kid's music states my name clearly. <u>Jaqi, they are gone.</u>

I open my eyes and realize I see only the running lights of the cockpit.

And it's not just Kid's music. It's blending with what Kalia says. "Jaqi, they're gone!"

<u>What happened?</u>

The music swells, and I can sense it, feel it, see it. All across the Dark Zone, Shir turn their massive bodies and move into the nodes, toward the memory of what they were.

They are not meant to go back.

Their bodies are shredded, torn apart, wreckage spread across every node in the universe.

But as they die, they sing. For the first time in a thousand years, they sing.

They remember, they *know* what they were, just for a second.

And then the devils are gone.

"Jaqi!" I don't even hear what Kalia says. I collapse

to the ground of the cockpit, soaked in sweat, laughing, maybe crying, maybe doing both. Kalia's on the transmitter and shouting the good news. More voices are coming through. Thuzerian voices, cross voices, hell, I think I hear even Z's voice again—but then one voice comes through I recognize.

"Araskar?" I say. That ragged, slurring voice, talking around the part of his tongue someone shot off. "That you?"

After a long moment, he comes back on the radio. "It is."

"How are you, slab?"

"Not dead yet."

"You are in deep shit," I say.

"I noticed."

"That en't what I—we'll talk." And then I drop limply to the floor of the cockpit, half crying, half laughing. And, I realize after a moment, surprised by what's coming out of my own mouth, singing. Singing for my mother, and all the forgotten dead.

21

Araskar

OUR CHILD HAS JAQI'S EYES. The minute she looks around the room, I can tell. Open, bright, inquisitive. You could mistake her for scared, but you would be wrong. She's examining everything, from under her fuzzy crop of hair, her chubby little arms moving as if she still expects to be pushing against the inside of her mother's womb. I half expect her to ask me if there's any fresh veggies left, aiya.

I put my big, scarred finger in the little tiny hand, and the tiny brown fingers close on it. Her little clouded eyes look at me, and she twitches.

"You know me?" I say. "You recognize my voice?"

Our child twitches again, kicks out unthinkingly, but the swaddling wrapped around her legs keeps her contained.

"You know me?"

She looks up at me, almost like she's saying *yes*. I think—no guarantee, mind you, but I think I see recognition in those eyes.

The music sweeps through me. A faint whistle, like a low organ, a rumbling like a piano in the distance, a shimmer of cymbals, and soaring melody like some instrument called down from heaven.

"Doing great," the doctor tells me. It's the first time I've seen a Thuzerian without a mask, exposing a scaly Sska face. They will remove them for sacred events, like a birth, and given that she's just midwifed the birth of a confirmed Saint's child, this event seems to have qualified as sacred enough. "Four hours of labor is a lot for a cross. We were worried."

Jaqi and I have been sequestered during the last few months of the pregnancy—not much to do but talk to the ever-growing bulge in her middle. Now, Jaqi is lying down while the orderlies check her over—and over, and over, because they still seem to think she turned to glass when she became a confirmed Saint—for any damage from childbirth.

"Yeah," I say, not really listening. Our daughter's eyes flicker up toward the ceiling, down again toward me. Now she's just back to being a confused little baby.

But for a moment there, we knew each other.

"Bring her over, Araskar, aiya?" Jaqi says, her voice soaked with exhaustion.

"Here she is," I say, walking to the bed. Jaqi blinks up at me, her eyes half lidded.

"Hey there, fella. Hey there, little girl." The baby curls up against her and paws at her breast, and Jaqi slips her breast out of the frock the doctors have given her, tries to get the baby to latch on. The little girl stares cross-eyed and opens her mouth and falls on the nipple. She tries like mad to fit the entire thing in her mouth, straining at it half-blind.

It's beautiful.

God, I never thought I'd see this. Birth, to me, is an adult body being yanked from a vat, hooked up to a dump and absorbing information straight into the brain. At my birth, I got vacuumed down, and given a data dump about the glorious struggle of the Empire against the Dark Zone. By the afternoon, I was at the shooting range, making sure the data dump worked for target practice.

There was even more goo, and plenty of blood, this time, but it was like watching something from another plane.

"Got her mater's appetite, ai?" Jaqi says. "Come on now. Latch on there. You can do it."

The Sska orderly seems a little fascinated by the lactation. Not standard for her people, I'd guess. "Be patient. Even for crosses, this may take some time to settle into a normal nursing pattern."

"How you feeling?" I ask.

"Hungry already," Jaqi says. "Nurse, you got anything that en't protein packs?"

"I can look," the nurse says, with a resigned air. She is used to these requests from Jaqi.

I take my new guitar from the corner and pick at two very slow, subdued chords. I know more chords now, but I'm trying to give the baby some mood music for nursing.

"Come on, there, little Dina," Jaqi says.

"Dina?" I ask. "You naming her already?"

"Dina was my mother's name," Jaqi says. "I reckon it works for a girl."

I want her to be able to choose her own name, when she gets older, like I did. But as Jaqi points out, and has pointed out many time, she wants something to call the little girl when she's toddling off.

"Dina," I say.

It feels right.

I put the guitar down and collapse into a chair nearby. I can't help noticing that everything aches more than it used to. And hanging out with Jaqi means that I don't fold as well—we've been eating good, and my middle bulges when I sit.

Not that I would trade it for what I had before.

I blink, and realize I've just slept an hour or so, and the orderly is standing by my side.

"The Minister wishes to congratulate you."

Kalia is fourteen years old and has changed, too. Something about those symbionts advanced parts of her aging process, but I suspect that governing in the madness of a war-torn galaxy has aged her all the faster. "How is she?" Kalia looks over at Jaqi.

"Sleeping, looks like," I say. Kalia and I creep to the bed and I peel back the blanket to get a look at Dina's face. The little baby's cloud of hair is all dry now, and her lips are pressed together, folded together.

"Aww," Kalia says, tracing a finger softly along one baby cheek. "She was so worried about the labor, but it sounds like it went fine."

"Yeah," I say, and then laugh. "Well, she screamed and threw a couple of things, and she bled a lot and there were other strange bodily fluids. All my instincts told me to draw my sword."

Jaqi blinks and says sleepily, "Kalia, girl, I put a sign on the door. DO NOT DISTURB. I read the words myself and everything. And they made sense. Sounded like they was spelled. Unlike half them words you folk write down."

"Sorry!" Kalia whispers. "I just wanted to see the baby." She leans over and watches Dina sleep a moment longer. Can't blame her.

I kiss Jaqi on the head and Dina as well, as gently as I can, and escort Kalia to the door.

"I need to speak to you in the situation room," Kalia says to me.

"Ah, damn it, can't it wait?"

"I told you it would wait until after the baby was born," Kalia says. "The baby's born."

I think about saying *no,* but I don't, because this is the kind of person Kalia's become.

We leave the birthing room and go a few steps down the hallway. The communicator on the wall is disabled, but still, Kalia's got a small, scrambled-frequency comm on the table. And a blanket in the chair. She's been sleeping here.

Toq is in here too, and he runs to me. "Araskar! Did you have a baby!"

I pick the little guy up. "I did. Her name, at least for now, is Dina."

"I want to see the baby!"

"Let Jaqi sleep, Toq," Kalia says, sounding every bit the annoyed older sister.

His face falls. "You can wake her up, Toq," I say. "She won't mind seeing you again."

"See?" he says to Kalia.

"If Araskar says it's all right, Araskar can deal with Jaqi's wrath," Kalia says, and motions her brother to go.

It's the most human Kalia's been in a while.

She settles into a chair, flicks the holo. Father Rixinius's face comes up. He's still nursing a wound from the battle that kept us from Irithessa a week ago.

"Praise to God and all the Saints, including our newest confirmed Saint, Saint Jaqi the Lightbringer. Our fleet continues rearguard action against the Resistance forces at Galactic Center. We will soon move to the location we discussed"—that's one of the disused nodes nobody but Jaqi knows about—"and with God's help, we will assault Irithessa again, once we have resupplied."

This is the first I've heard of this. My heart sinks. I knew it was possible, but it's bad news all the same. "The attack on Irithessa failed."

"The blockade is still too strong. The Resistance still controls Keil, and they can make ships and soldiers faster than we can."

Kalia speaks up, adding to Rixinius. "If John Starfire is alive, like the rumors say, he's still got a thriving movement waiting for him."

"He's dead. What are you going to do with the prisoner?"

Kalia doesn't answer, an answer of itself. I can almost hear her saying, *Whatever the hell I want*. Not that Kalia would ever admit to that. She reaches down and grips the guns that sit naturally at her waist, massages the grip in a way that reminds me too much of John Starfire and his soulsword.

"You can't prosecute Aranella," I say. "Not now."

"Just because she saved your life—"

"She made the operation against the Shir at Rocina possible. Without her, those mothering triads would have been busy elsewhere. We could have lost ten star systems, not four, before Jaqi . . . did what she did. You've run the numbers."

"Aranella committed genocide," Kalia says, her voice dark. "Remember Shadow Sun Seven? We've found six other dark spots like that. Close to a hundred thousand people died in 'consolidation.' And that's what we know so far. The rest of the bluebloods from the central worlds have disappeared. Billions."

"I'm not arguing with that. I'm saying that we can't try war crimes as a coalition." I try not to let the desperation show in my voice.

"I agree with Father Rixinius. The Thuzerians' bylaws will have to do. There's precedent. We wouldn't be the first people to haul in war criminals under religious jurisdiction." The last time we talked about this Father Rixinius was there, and nodding right along with Kalia when she said, *Aranella is going to pay for the crimes of the Resistance.*

"No. I won't accept that. That's the first step in a religious autocracy."

"It is not."

The silence hangs between us, Kalia looking petulant. Sometimes I can reduce this girl to sounding like a normal teenager. Less and less lately, but sometimes I can.

Kalia speaks again. "You never should have promised to let her go free."

"There it is," I say. "Can't have a conversation without that."

"By what authority could you make a promise like that? She's just as guilty as her husband of war crimes. We deal with her, we show how we'll react to his return."

"John Starfire is dead," I say. "I shot him off a planet-cracker then blew up the planet underneath him. He's dead, all right?" Why does she always bring this up?

"You know what I believe."

I know. Kalia says that she has six reliable John Starfire sightings since Rocina.

It's nonsense. But as something between a missing, soon-to-return Chosen One and a martyr, John Starfire's become very useful for the Resistance. And Kalia's never hidden her disappointment at my failure to produce a corpse.

In the last five months of cross pregnancy and gestation, I've learned just how hard it is to change the reins of power within the galaxy.

The Reckoning is a movement, not a government, and all our allies—the Hukas, the Necros, the Thuzerians—aren't interested in forming anything more than a coalition. Well, each one wants a government, but they want something different. The Kurgul nests and the Necros would like a very weak confederation subject to bribes. The Thuzerians would like a strong central government. A religious one.

We don't want any of that. But we have to figure something out. The vats, as impossible as it sounds, are still running. The Resistance, depleted, with more than its share of defectors to the Reckoning, still believes and fights. We have the command of the nodes, but they have more ships every day. We'll win eventually—the crooks of the galaxy are on our side, and that's an advantage—but what then?

We'll have criminals on one side, religious warriors on the other, and the bluebloods—led by Kalia—in the middle.

"Aranella is more useful as a prisoner," I say.

She looks back up, and her face is that mask again, the mask she's gotten so used to making. "Aranella is never going free, Araskar. You had no right to make that promise. Our next destination is going to have to be the Thuzerians' system. It's the only place you can raise that child safely. For better or worse, that's where we'll try her."

I leave off saying anything there. If there is one thing Jaqi and I are very tired of, it's believers treating her like the Chosen One. Well, she's not tired of the part where they'll bring her fresh food whenever she asks, but otherwise . . .

"Sleep," Kalia says. "When you awaken, when Jaqi's strong enough, we'll go back to Llyrixa." It has an air of finality about it. "You two and the child will be safe there. I can finally relax."

"Kalia," I say, trying to keep the anger out of my voice. "You will never relax. Neither will I. We'll always be looking over our shoulder, one hand on our weapon. We'll always have the voices of the dead in our ears. You choose whether you listen to them, or you live."

"Don't tell me about the dead," Kalia snaps. "You're still a cross."

The room goes as silent as vacuum for a moment.

And then she's horrified. And she apologizes. And touches my hand, deliberately, tells me how tired she is. I nod along and say she's forgiven. I go back to the birthing room.

My mind's made up.

"Hey," Jaqi says, as I climb into the bed next to her. "You're looking like you just went a couple rounds with a Zarra."

"With Kalia," I say, and Jaqi groans. I lean in close to her, whisper in her ear. "Definitely not changing my mind now."

Jaqi stokes Dina's little cloud of hair. "I want this little girl to get raised normal, not in a monastery where folk treat her like she's made of glass."

"Me too." I nestle my head against Jaqi's shoulder. "I need to go see her."

"Her?" Jaqi looks back at me, her eyes bleary. "Now?"

"You think I'll get a chance when we're surrounded by Thuzerians?"

"Just keep your wits up, Araskar." She kisses me tiredly.

So I get up, and get dressed. Really dressed. Including the soulswords I don't like wearing anymore. And I walk through the ship. Our ship is under blackout and secrecy warnings tight enough to keep the fleet from knowing whether the Chosen One—Jaqi—is really even here. Which means it's not far to a prisoner who is also under blackout.

Aranella.

Vanaliel, now sporting a pair of synthskin-and-steel legs, guards her. She lights up when she sees me. Vanaliel was one of our most high-profile deserters. She's devoted her life to paying me back for saving her. "Araskar," she says. "I've asked to pray with her again."

"Didn't go for it, eh?"

"I used to think she had faith," Vanaliel says, shifting. "Not anymore." I nod. The victory has been good for the Thuzerians. They've attracted, for once, millions of converts and are opening up new monasteries on worlds all across the galaxy. Gives the Reckoning a few million new soldiers.

That worries us too.

"How's the legs?"

"Better than new." She dips her head, in just a hint of a bow. "Praise be to Saint Jaqi the Lightbringer. And the child."

"Saint Jaqi's got a few words for you."

"For me?" Vanaliel goes white. Her brush with death really affected this girl. "The Saint wishes to speak to me?"

"Yes," I say. "But not via a comm." I press my soulsword into Vanaliel's hands.

This is the big risk. Vanaliel's our one wild card in the plan. But I'm pretty familiar with Jaqi's ability to inspire people at this point.

So while Vanaliel speaks to Jaqi through the soulsword, I enter the cell. And Aranella turns and looks at me. That face. In the shadows, haggard from imprisonment, it looks even more like Rashiya's. "You're back."

"It's been a while," I say.

"I heard celebrating. Did you have your child?"

"Yes. Named her Dina. She's beautiful." I pause. "I understand."

Aranella doesn't answer.

"I understand what I did to you when I killed Rashiya."

"Araskar, I said I forgave you. What else do you want?"

"Peace." I close my eyes for a moment, open them again. "Even when they thought you had betrayed him, the Resistance respected you. I need you to go back and build a coalition. I need peace. The longer this war goes on, the louder the extremists get."

"You expect me to go back and preach this nonsense your Reckoning is spreading—that Jorians and humans were the same race?"

"Believe whatever the hell you want," I say. "Just respect the cease-fire."

"How are we supposed to get past your guard there?"

"The Saint has pull," I say.

Aranella laughs. "I remember the same moment with John. The moment when he decided to take advantage of his followers' faith, rather than try and run from what they wanted to put on him."

"Let me guess. It was the moment he changed forever."

"No," Aranella says, standing. "Just one of many small changes. To the day he died, he was still the man I married, Araskar. He believed. That was who he was."

And that's another thing that worries Jaqi. "Come on."

I step outside and face Vanaliel, whose face is streaked with tears. She hands the sword back to me. "I'll do what she asks."

Jaqi is never far from Taltus's old sword, and it was

more difficult to forge a connection between the two, but not impossible. The ship's ready?

Node'll open when I said.

We've planned this.

I hate what we have to do to Vanaliel. She'll be the one who deactivates the sensory network within our ship. She'll be the traitor at the highest level of her rank. She'll be the one who faces Kalia's wrath, and the wrath of all the other soldiers who believe as she does, because of what Jaqi and I asked. I saved her life because it was the right thing to do, not so I could call in a terrible favor.

I watch Vanaliel walk away, toward the sensor array.

And a moment later, I hear the telltale change in the hum of the systems that means the sensory block is in place.

"Let's go," I say to Aranella.

It's a relatively quiet walk to the cloaked hangar bay, where sits the shuttle that has been home to Jaqi and me for the last few months.

"You'll broadcast Sanctuary Acts refugee codes on every channel the minute you leave the node," I say. "I assume they'll be very interested in a stolen Thuzerian shuttle."

She nods, looks between me and the shuttle.

"I hope you find your children," I say. "Aranella. I really do."

And then the strangest thing in all the universe. She embraces me.

I didn't expect this one. Aranella's not very good at hugging me. She's stiff as a blade, her arms awkwardly wrapping around my back.

I start to pull away. "I uh . . . I didn't expect—"

That's when she yanks out my short soulsword, and stabs me.

I lurch backward, grab my long soulsword, draw it halfway, but by then she's stabbed me three times.

That's strange.

I'm so soft.

And it hurts. More than any other wound I've taken.

I stumble back, bleeding like mad from the gut wounds. I've got my sword out, but Aranella is already stepping back.

"I'll give you your peace. But I lied about forgiving you. My daughter's memories deserve their rest."

And then she's in the ship.

And I'm on the ground, bleeding from three deep stab wounds.

Not dead yet. Not dead yet. Plenty of time. Plenty of time, like I told my daughter. I drag myself across the metal floor, to a safe point away from the ignition of the shuttle, leaving blood and offal and probably pieces of my guts on the floor. Not dead yet. Just cut my guts. And by the amount of blood, maybe a few crucial arteries. I don't have to examine it. My whole chest is aflame with pain.

But not dead yet.

This would be a stupid way to die anyway. I took Irithessa with the Resistance. I fought the Shir. I . . . I can't remember what else I've done but I'm sure this would be a stupid way to die.

I just need to slap the emergency protocol door opener.

The emergency protocol that Vanaliel disabled.

It's all right. I can tell Jaqi. I've got my sword in my hand—no wait, I dropped it when I fell. Did I? It's hard to see. The light of the shuttle is washing everything out. I think I see the soulsword over there. I crawl along the ground.

I'm crawling, aren't I? I can't tell if I'm crawling or holding still now. I think my arms are moving.

It's all right. Not dead yet.

Like I told Dina, we have lots of time.

All the time in the universe.

22

Jaqi

I NEVER THOUGHT I would have a normal life. I hoped. And hope is a dangerous thing in the wild worlds.

I looked in Dina's little eyes not a couple of hours ago and I reckoned that was all the hope in the universe. I saw Araskar sitting next to me, thought about how I was really coming to love that sour dude with the scars on his face and how I reckoned we'd be slightly better parents than I thought, and I didn't mind that I was giving into scary hope.

Now I'm looking down at Araskar, in an evil big puddle of blood, and not moving. Not moving one burning bit. Turning a funny blue color. Because of what we planned. Because we thought any peace was better than the Red Peace, which, despite me doing a heap of miracles, keeps getting redder and redder.

"Jaqi, you should come away," Kalia says. "I cannot—"

"Leave me alone." I bend over him, touch his body, and start wondering how exactly I can bring him back. I done it with Z, and Z done explained it to me. I en't made a new node since I made the one inside Z, but there's got to be some of them nano-Suits out there.

<u>Kid,</u> I say to the music in the back of my head. <u>Kid, you there?</u>

The music is strained, like the instruments are on the verge of detuning. Kid gave birth today too, and is tired, although I don't reckon there's words for Kid's version of them feelings.

<u>Kid, I need to open up one of them micro-nodes inside this fella and bring through what can fix him.</u>

The music stops. It's never stopped before. <u>Kid!</u>

After a moment, that music, a kind of complicated, low, pulsing thing. Kid can't do it right now.

<u>Yes it can!</u> I yell back. I reach out for the music, try to seize it, pour it down into Araskar. <u>Come on now!</u>

I sing my mother's field song, and my own voice sounds funny to me. I sing it and I grab the music and pour it into Araskar and imagine a tiny, microscopic node bringing tiny Suits through . . . only there en't no more nano-Suits, is there?

"Jaqi."

"Bugger off," I say, and then realize who I've said it to.

Z crouches in front of me. His new tattoos blur. Why? Why am I seeing through these blurred eyes? Something wrong with my eyes?

"Z, I need some of those fellas what's in your blood," I say, and rub my face, getting Araskar's blood on it. "Them nano-Suits."

Z touches my hand with his own bloody one. "Jaqi, I cannot offer you this. I am sorry."

"What? You always talking about blood and honor, you can't spare some blood?"

"I would pour out all my blood to save Araskar," Z says. "He is a valiant companion, your paramour, and it is my place to kill him anyway, as he took my honor. But the nano-Suits have gone from me. I gave them over to my people, to heal them from the virus that ravaged them. They went among my family, and then among my clan, and then among other clans, scattering across all of Zarra-krr-Zar, for those who chose survival as a type of honor. Every last nano-Suit has gone to use."

"They're on your Zarra world? I can summon them?"

"The nano-Suits were exhausted of their capabilities. Few still function."

"That's okay! It's evil worth a shot—"

He grunts, and I hate how I know what he'll say. "I fear it is too late for Araskar, Jaqi. I had only been dead a few moments when you brought through the Suits on the moon of Trace. He has lain here long, and lost too much blood."

"No!" I shake my head. "No, hell no! He went through

so much, Z. This is wrong. Evil wrong." I don't say what I think—*and our own fault.*

He thought Aranella had let go of her grudge. He believed her. It's why we took that chance of shutting down the communication on the ship. We had it all planned. It was going to work, because he kept saying *I believe Aranella.*

"Let me carry him," Z says. "Let me bear his honor."

I huddle on the floor while Z picks up Araskar, heedless of the blood that soon soaks him, and carries the body of my child's father, the fella I loved.

"This was supposed to be a happy day." I feel so damn stupid saying it.

Hope is a dangerous thing in the wild worlds, but I hoped so badly.

A day passes, and an eternity. I nurse Dina and hold her and don't let no one else touch her. Other folk talk to me. I blink and stare, and go back to holding my baby. Toq comes in and cries. Z comes in and doesn't speak, just holds my hand in his big, freshly tattooed one. I just sit there with my baby.

Dina cries and I change her diaper and we start to get the hang of the nursing business, and finally once she's asleep I get dressed and wrap her up on my chest.

And Araskar's not there. Keep waiting for that slab to come through the door and grimace and mumble something about how he can't find any more chocolate in the entire galaxy, will I ever stop asking, how'm I feeling?

The door never opens.

I go to Kalia in the situation-room. She's sitting there touching the guns she got from Scurv, closing her eyes like she's talking to them.

"Kalia," I say, and she snaps out of it.

"Jaqi, you're up. How are you feeling?"

I en't got time for this. "Kalia, I'm going away."

"What? You can't go away—the whole galaxy is on fire. And everyone will be looking for you. We need you to keep our advantage with the nodes, so we can beat the Resistance—"

"You en't going to beat the Resistance," I say. "Not without some kind of give. Not without peace. I wish we could smash them for good, because they deserve it, but that's just how it is." I don't say, *I'm done with hope,* but I think it.

"Jaqi. Come on. What about Quinn? What about Bill? What about everyone who died on Shadow Sun Seven? What about—"

"Out the airlock with that, Kalia," I snap. "I did my bit for the lost. You know what's in the future. Just more war."

"Not if we play our hand right."

"They have the vats. They have the shipyards. They have more dreadnoughts and troops coming off the line every day. You have to try and make peace with..." I can't say her name.

"The woman who killed Araskar? The woman who put my mother in some black site labor camp, and I still haven't found her?"

"She's a vile piece of space," I say. "Any justice, and she'd be out the airlock. But she don't believe her husband was no Son of Stars. She don't believe like the rest of the Resistance." I swallow against the raggedy lump that threatens to shoot out my throat in a sob. "En't no easy answers in a way."

Kalia takes a moment, now. I can see the changes in her already. See the way she touches the Scurv-guns, like they is the ones that understand her. I reckon they do understand her. They just spit out heat, and anger. "I don't care what Aranella believes. They have to be beaten. Humiliated. The entire galaxy needs to see you with your foot on John Starfire's throat."

That sounds familiar, ai, though I can't say why. "And then? Even if you beat them, how much you reckon another Resistance springs up? The bluebloods spent a thousand years ruling the galaxy; you'll find folks who still resent you. Another fight. And another. When peace comes, it'll be your choice."

"Stop," she says.

"Galaxy had a never-ending war for a thousand years.

Had an Empire lived off the business of eternal war. Make the choice now, aiya?"

"You don't understand," she says. "You're still a cross."

I swallow my words, and clutch Dina against my breast. "Reckon I deserve that. Given what I said to you, back on the moon of Trace one time."

"You do deserve it." Kalia bites off the words. "You'll never understand."

"I'm just a spaceways scab, aiya?"

The door buzzes. "Oh hell," Kalia says. "I didn't want to do this now."

Two soldiers stand there with Vanaliel, her arms bound. Her face is red. She's been weeping, more weeping than even Dina done this morning.

Kalia looks at Vanaliel, and nods at the guards, who withdraw from the room, leaving the three of us together.

Whether she notices it or not, Kalia's hand goes to one of her guns. "What do you have to say to Jaqi, traitor?"

"I . . ." Vanaliel can barely speak. "The Saint's consort asked it of me. Araskar. He asked me, for the loyalty I bear him from the battle of Rocina. I am no traitor."

"I know," I say. "I planned it with him. More fool me."

Kalia clutches the handle of the gun at her waist and narrows her eyes, looking on Vanaliel. "You have committed worse treason than I could imagine."

I step in front of Vanaliel, holding my baby, and for half

a second all my guts, which don't feel so good after giving birth anyway, churn up because I see that look in Kalia, the look I last saw on a catwalk high on an Archive Tower, that look that says murder.

"I'm leaving, Kalia," I say. I take Vanaliel by the arm. "This one'll come with me, to serve as my bodyguard. That's her sentence for what she's done, aiya?"

"You're not leaving."

"One day you'll figure out that you need peace. Real peace. Without the red." I hate that it's ending like this, but I turn to leave.

"You told me something once," Kalia says, stopping me. "That you couldn't run anymore. That you had given up on a normal life, and you had to fight."

"That's what I figured on, when this fight began," I say. "But now I've seen the other end of it. I seen what happens when there's no end to the fight. This little girl deserves a normal life. Deserves to have her mama come when she calls, and at least know where her daddy's laid to rest."

I reach for the door's sensor.

Kalia draws a gun—and points it at me.

Oh shit.

"You don't leave, Jaqi."

"You gonna shoot me, and the babe too?" I sound a hell of a lot more confident than I feel. I didn't figure she'd do this. But a part of me wonders. Those guns don't miss.

"If I can't have a Saint, I'll have a martyr."

I wet my lips. "That's a hell of a thing to say." And a moment later, I add, "Go on, then. I'll be just as dead as Quinn."

Kalia lets out a roar like any Zarra.

And shoots the table.

Dina screams at the noise. The table breaks into a dozen pieces of warped plasticene, rebounding off the walls. I cover all of Dina and yell, "Aiya, Kalia, I got a baby here!"

"I hate them so much," Kalia says, and suddenly she's just a fourteen-year-old girl, crying her eyes out. "I hate them so much. I hate them so much that it's exhausting." She sobs and sobs, and a dam breaks inside me, and I cry too, and then Dina joins us, and I figure we en't shed near enough tears yet anyway.

After a long time, I pull away and we stare into each other's puffy eyes.

"You ought to come with me too," I say.

"I've got an armistice to work on." She says each word like it's been pulled from her throat by a hook.

"You mean that?"

"I do," she says. "I have to."

———————

The shuttle waits for us. I walk across the hangar, my throat still raw. Must have stayed there holding Kalia for an eternity.

I think she'll do okay.

I still don't know whether I'm doing the right thing. That's the bit about being the Oogie of Stars that's toughest of all, and I reckon the part that undid John Starfire. See, when it turns out that "Son of Stars" just means "real good with nodes," I don't get no special guidance from God. Kid en't quite a god—vi's got all the power and none of the sense. I get the same judgment anyone else does.

I could be wrong. Aranella lied about forgiving Araskar, that much seems true, and she could be lying about wanting peace. But Araskar believed that she had really turned against her husband. And the memories I took from John Starfire support it. Aranella cared about her surviving children. More than she cared about the Resistance.

I know what that feels like. I want Dina to live that normal life. Might be that's selfish, might be that's me thinking of myself before the cause. But I want her to call and hear her mommy answer, until the day I'm an old crone and she comes when I call.

Kalia made me promise to read the Bible someday, so I got that tucked into my knapsack, along with every bit of fresh fruit, nuts, and vegetables I could steal on this ship. I already been snacking on it, walking toward the ship.

"You actually wish me to go with you?" Vanaliel asks.

"Yep, I need a good sword arm watching out for the babe." She's a fine slab herself, but I don't add that bit.

Vanaliel wipes her running nose and bows—that bowing again! "I will be with you until death, Saint—"

"Easy, girl," I say. "You got to relax. First order is to take it easy. No bowing."

"Yes, Saint Jaqi." I see her muscles straining, trying not to bow.

And then another voice. "Jaqi."

"Z." I turn around and see the big fella. "Thanks for what you did. Loading up his body and all."

"Do not thank me," he says. "I did what honor demanded."

Same old Z. I give him a serious hug, although I have to lean into him a bit to keep from squishing Dina, where she's sleeping in a wrap on my chest.

"Don't suppose you want to come?" I whisper.

"I will stay with you for a while yet," he says, and my heart does a jump. "I must return to my people eventually. But as my honor is still lost, so perhaps I will find it in a strange galaxy. And it is my duty to help lay Araskar in the ground of his home planet."

"Thanks, big fella. Blood and honor."

He clutches my hand. "You are a nursing mother. It is proper now to say blood, honor, and breast milk."

"Is it?" I am looking forward to life on a ship with this weirdo.

We turn toward the ship and I hear a shout from behind me. "Jaqi!"

I turn around and see Toq. The kid is just standing in the middle of the hangar, his face crumpled up and about to cry.

"Kalia know you're out here?" I ask.

He doesn't answer. Just runs to me and wraps his little arms around me. "Don't leave me here. I want to see Earth."

Aw . . . hell. "Does your sister know?"

"I want to see Earth. Then we can tell her."

"How'd you know that's where we were going?"

"I didn't. You just told me."

"You're too clever a kid."

He clings to me, not saying anything. I sigh. I reckon I better get used to this. "Fine, you come along, but you promise me you'll head to bed when I say so."

"You sound just like my mom."

I don't move for a minute, because that thing's back in my throat. "I guess that's a good start, aiya."

Coda

THE PLANET EARTH WAS steeped with the memory of life.

Its oceans had risen, lowered, locked into ice and melted again. Cities fell, their towers reduced to spurs and skeletons. Grass grew over twenty billion graves. Deer grazed in the hearts of cities; jaguars and eagles prowled the empty steel structures.

Still it waited.

Once twenty billion humans had walked this planet, singing and writing and making love and dying. They founded empires, and marveled at the speed of boats, of trains, of spaceships, of the power they could have when they joined together. They found reasons to hate each other, and their empires fell and other empires rose again. They found ways to change themselves. They found creatures so different from themselves they could not perceive them in their true state, but they joined with those creatures and crossed the great gulf of the stars.

A tiny, but persistent, virus undid them.

A few humans survived, but forgot their star-spanning Empire, save in a few old tales of travelers to the sky. For them, Earth had become a vast, empty world, and they stayed inside their walls and feared ghosts.

Earth remembered. Earth waited for the travelers to come home.

On a hill above an ocean, in what had once been the greatest city in the world, and was now simply a stand of trees, the first node opened.

The woman, lanky, still stooped and weary from childbirth, stepped through. The light from Earth's star shone on her deep brown skin, on the skin of the child that she cradled against her breast.

She was followed by another child. A boy. Then two hulking figures, man and woman, who carried a shrouded, unmoving figure—and two spades.

On that hill, they dug. Dug until they were coated with sweat and dust, until the hole was deep enough for the tallest to stand in, and there they buried the shrouded body. The two largest figures maneuvered the body into the ground, and cast the dirt onto it.

The first woman knelt over the hole, and said, "I reckon you finally came home. It en't much, but it's what I could do for you. This little girl will know where her daddy lies." She pulled the shroud aside, and traced the scars on the dead man's face. "You lived well."

And her tears fell onto Earth's surface, with the dirt that filled the grave.

After they finished, the baby turned toward the sun, blinked, and stretched. Her mother gently rubbed the child's soft cheek.

"Nice place, aiya?" she said to the others. "Let's find something to eat."

Acknowledgments

And then there were three. With even more people to thank since *A Red Peace* released.

I owe it all to Beth Meacham, who believed in this project when it was a few rough pages, when it was one novel, and when it was a three-book proposal. Sara Megibow is a giant among agents, and Katharine and Mordicai did a wonderful job publicizing Starfire. Thanks to Kameron Hurley, Mary Robinette Kowal, and Beth Cato for great blurbs, and the *Barnes & Noble Sci-Fi & Fantasy Blog* people for the promotion. Thanks to Wendy Wagner (the best tour buddy!), Duane at University Bookstore, and the crew at Village Books, Barnes & Noble Eugene, and the Book Bin for the Starfire events. Thanks to everyone involved with Cascade Writers and Codex Writers, with special mention of my Obi-Wan, Eric James Stone.

Thanks to the readers who enjoyed *A Red Peace* and *Shadow Sun Seven* and got the word out.

Langley Hyde continues to be Starfire Beta Reader Supreme, wading through a half-finished, mostly bracketed nonsense draft with a keen eye and Blade of Biggerify. She turns up the stakes and kicks out the jams. (In this metaphor, the jams are better metaphors.)

Big hugs and thanks to Khaalidah Mohammed-Ali, my sister in swashbuckling, for a fun blow-off-steam project between homework. Thanks especially to Effie Seiberg, Cory Skerry, Sean Patrick Kelley, Joey Elmer, Rebecca Mablango-Mayor, Rachael K. Jones, and my wonderful coworkers and students at Northwest Indian College for support and sanity.

All credit and love to my parents and siblings for years of support, from Super Tiger till now. Thanks to my children for their patience with a writer dad. You deserve a better world than we're giving you, but we're doing what we can.

Everything good happens because of Chrissy, and so I end with enough love to fuel a thousand stars.

About the Author

Photograph by Chrissy Ellsworth

SPENCER ELLSWORTH's short fiction has previously appeared in *Lightspeed*, *The Magazine of Fantasy & Science Fiction*, and *Tor.com*. He is the author of the Starfire trilogy, which begins with *Starfire: A Red Peace*. He lives in the Pacific Northwest with his wife and three children, works as a teacher/administrator at a small tribal college on a Native American reservation, and blogs at spencerellsworth.com.

TOR·COM

Science fiction. Fantasy. The universe.

And related subjects.

*

More than just a publisher's website, *Tor.com*
is a venue for **original fiction, comics,** and

discussion of the entire field of SF and fantasy,

in all media and from all sources. Visit our site

today — and join the conversation yourself.